THE TAXIDERMIST

Part I & II

Joey Dolton

Boro Publishing, LLC

Copyright © 2024 Joey Dolton

Copyright © 2024 Joey Dolton All rights reserved
The characters and events portrayed in this book are fictitious. Any similarity to real persons, living or dead, is coincidental and not intended by the author.

No part of this book may be reproduced, or stored in a retrieval system, or transmitted in any form or by any means, electronic, mechanical, photocopying, recording, or otherwise, without express written permission of the publisher.

ISBN-13 (Kindle): 979-8-9898592-3-8
ISBN-13 (Paperback): 979-8-9898592-4-5 ISBN-13 (Hard Cover): 979-8-9898592-5-2

Cover design by: Joey Dolton
Library of Congress Control Number: 2024903950
Printed in the United States of America

To Family, who make everything possible

CONTENTS

Title Page
Copyright
Dedication
PART I   1
CHAPTER 1   2
CHAPTER 2   16
CHAPTER 3   28
CHAPTER 4   41
CHAPTER 5   54
CHAPTER 6   68
CHAPTER 7   75
CHAPTER 8   87
CHAPTER 9   101
CHAPTER 10   117
CHAPTER 11   134
CHAPTER 12   144

CHAPTER 13	155
PART II	168
CHAPTER 14	169
CHAPTER 15	178
CHAPTER 16	187
CHAPTER 17	195
CHAPTER 18	203
CHAPTER 19	212
CHAPTER 20	222
EPILOGUE	233
About The Author	235
Books By This Author	237

PART I

CHAPTER 1

Origins

THEY SAY TRUE BEAUTY comes from the inside, but Vincent Greenwood couldn't agree less with this statement. In his humble opinion, beauty was outside and only skin deep. However, before he is to be condemned for this opinion, he does have a good reason. Vincent Greenwood is a taxidermist, a well renown one at that, known for his hyper-realistic displays.

Bears, foxes, wolfs, even monkey's, he has done them all. Yet it just wasn't enough. He wasn't sure why, he was just missing something. It was like an itch that couldn't be stopped. For now, however, he was content with his work, or at least, he was until the incident happened.

One day, early in the morning, Vincent was driving home from a late-night charity auction selling some of his art. Some of these pieces included a recreation of dogs playing poker, Napoleon the pig, and steamboat Willie. The auction had been a major success, and the money raised was going to a good cause. However, the auction had also had an open bar, and Vincent had a few too many drinks. In the morning, he was paying the price.

As he was driving home, Vincent was still slightly tipsy. Despite his inebriated state, he tried to be as careful as possible to avoid the ire of the cops. The roads were dark, empty, and lonely. Not a single person was out and about, or at least, he thought there weren't. In a split second, he was proved wrong.

Out of nowhere, a figure had darted across the street. This figure was a person, a young woman. Vincent didn't have much time to react, as his car slammed into her, her body being sent flying.

Vincent stopped his vehicle and got out to see if he could help. She was a brunette, her hair in a ponytail, and was dressed in exercise gear, likely jogging early in the morning. She was currently lying a few feet away, not moving. Vincent walked over to her.

"Hey lady, are you okay?" He said, lightly slapping her cheek. "I didn't mean to run you over. I was driving fine, honest."

The woman did not respond, her head simply loling over. Vincent reached down and tried to find her pulse, but found nothing. She was dead.

"Oh God, what do I do, what do I do." He began to panic. If he was caught, he'd go to prison for sure.

It was at this point, that he noticed that the young woman was quite beautiful, and on the outside, she didn't look injured at all, it must of been internal injuries. Her green eyes stared through him lifelessly however, confirming her true state. It would be a shame if she were to be buried, all that beauty lost to the world forever. Plus, he also didn't want to go to prison. It was at that point that an idea came to him, a truly devious one at that.

Vincent was a taxidermist. He could preserve the young woman, and put her someplace no one would ever find her. No one would know what happened to her except for him, and this would solve both his dilemmas at the same time.

Looking around, he saw no one. He knew if anyone came by on the road, it would be all over, but he knew he couldn't rush this. Carefully, he peeled the young woman's body off of the road and stuffed it into his trunk. He was glad the woman was slim, or else he wouldn't be able to fit her in.

Once that was done, he drove her body back to his home. This took a while, as he wanted to avoid the most heavily used roads, save he get pulled over. Eventually he got home and pulled into his garage and opened the trunk.

The girl's body was still there, and Vincent breathed both a sigh of relief and panic. He had killed her and taken her body. He was committed now and had to do this; he had no choice. Picking up the young woman, he carried her down into his basement. Here he kept his equipment and the various animal skins he had preserved. He laid her body on a table and went to work.

He began by undressing the young woman, carefully removing her clothes and leaving her in only her bra and panties. He had no intentions of perverting her, he simply didn't want to ruin her clothing. She was thin, but not to the point where it was unhealthily. She had the perfect physique, a body that any model would kill for. Something he had literally done to her.

Her face was soft, yet stern and mature. She had high cheek bones and a small nose. He grabbed her face his hands and turned her head side to side to check out her profile.

Yes, she was truly a lovely sight, and it was a shame her life had to end. She didn't seem to be much older than nineteen, and had her whole life ahead of her. He wished he knew her name, but he had a job to do.

He started by taking photos of the corpse for reference, and then began taking measurements. Next, he began to wash her body. He had to make sure she was was clean, otherwise it could attract bacteria and mold, and cause the process to fail.

The young woman had a smooth stomach, and Vincent could feel the firmness and softness. She clearly did yoga or something along those lines.

He moved down her legs and began rubbing the soap. They were long, yet not disproportionate to the rest of her body. He was starting to really feel a connection with this woman, and wondered what her personality was like.

After a few more minutes of washing, he dried her off. Then, using his tools, he began to prep her for preservation. He was a bit nervous. Taxidermy was a very delicate art, and the slightest misstep could cause it all to fall apart. He was also not experienced with human subjects, so this was a first for him.

Luckily for Vincent, she was a fresh cadaver, meaning her skin was still smooth and had not yet begun to break down. It made his job easier, but there was still a lot of work to do.

He took great care in each step, making sure his work was perfect. After all, he didn't want to have a bad looking exhibit in his home. He began by drawing the blood from her body. Once this was done, she looked pale white. It was time for the next step.

Vincent held his knife in his hands. He knew there was no coming back from this. He had to preserve her, but she was still a human being. "I'm sorry miss. It's a shame you had to die this way." He squeezed her hand before he began his work.

Vincent was skilled at taxidermy, and he was no beginner. However, he was used to deer and bears, where there were less custom features to get right. This was a human woman. He had to cut through her skin and muscle with great precision, so as not to damage anything.

It took him hours to finish, and when he was done, the woman's skin was completely peeled from her body. All that remained was her red flesh. Before he could dispose of this however, he began to make a cast of what remained so he could have something to put her skin on. While this dried, he began the process of tanning her skin.

Tanning was an important step in taxidermy, as without it, the skin would decompose. The process was simple, and Vincent had refined his process through the years. However, he still needed to take great care so as to not ruin the skin. He didn't want her to come out looking like leather. While the tanning process took place and the cast dry, all he could do is wait, alone with his thoughts.

Vincent was a good person, at least in his own mind. He was always generous to charities, and was kind to animals, both the wild and domesticated. He never had a cruel bone in his body, and he loved the people of the world, no matter their race, yet he enjoyed this process.

As the hours ticked by, he thought more and more about the young woman's fate. What was her life like? Was she a student, or a worker, or both? Who were her parents? How would they react to the news of her death and disappearance? Would she have a funeral?

His thoughts went wild, and his imagination was running wild. It was like a storybook, where a man had committed an unspeakable crime, and now had to live with the consequences.

He didn't care for his actions, as he had done what he had to. Yet, he shouldn't shake the pleasure he had felt while doing it. He loved it. He could not deny this, there was no point. He wanted more. He wanted to do this again and wanted to improve his craft.

When the tanning process was finished, he returned and removed the cast, and was pleased to see it had hardened. He had to remove this, then use it to create a plastic mold of her body on which to attach her skin. Once the cast was off, he took it to a machine that made the plastic molds for his taxidermied work. She was going to be a lot bigger piece than most of his work, save for the bears.

He made sure the mold was perfect, and once it was, he went back to her flesh, and began to cut it away to reveal her bones. He would need this to get a proper structure, after all, what was better to support her preserved form that what had supported her living form?

It was hard work, and by the time he was done, Vincent was drenched in sweat, and it was pitch black outside. He left the reassembled skeleton to dry.

He went upstairs, and cleaned himself off, and ate dinner. It had been a long day, and he was tired. As he drifted off to sleep, he knew that in the morning, his work would continue.

As he lay in bed, he couldn't help but think about what he had done. What he had done to her. He had taken her life away, sure it was accident, but he still did it. He denied her family closure for his own selfish purposes. But the worst thing? He enjoyed it. He was enjoying taking this young woman and preserving her, and wanted it do it again. He needed to prove he could do it again.

As these thoughts filled his head, Vincent Greenwood drifted off to sleep.

Vincent awoke the next morning, and his thoughts still lingered. He tried to go through his normal routine; he got the paper, ate breakfast, and read today's news. As he read through it, he saw it. A picture of the woman downstairs.

The headline was simple, a young woman was missing. It didn't say how long, but from what Vincent could guess, she had been reported missing last night. He continued reading.

According to the article, her name was Emily Lyon, and she was nineteen years old. She was a student at a local college. The article said that the police were conducting a thorough investigation, and were asking for the public to come forward if they had any information.

Vincent's eyes darted across the page, drinking in the details. Emily was a bright, young girl, and was studying medicine at the local university. She had a strong moral code, and wanted to change the world for the better. She was kind, and was always volunteering at various events and fundraisers.

Her parents, George and Amanda, were distraught at her disappearance. They stated that they had not seen or heard from her since the night before, and were worried sick. They were asking anyone with any information on her whereabouts to come forward.

Vincent was stunned. He had taken the life of such a sweet and kind young woman, and he had enjoyed it. It was a sobering thought, and it caused him to reflect on his own actions. But as he reflected, he could not bring himself to regret them. He knew that he had done the right thing, and that Emily was in a better place now. He also knew that no one would ever discover her true fate, and that made him smile.

It was at that moment, that Vincent Greenwood knew what he had to do. He had to finish his project. He had to finish Emily.

He raced downstairs and was greeted by the sight of her. Her beautiful skeleton was staring at him, though her skull obviously held no emotions. She was a pure, untouched, and beautiful thing, and he would make her into a goddess. He set out and began his work once more.

The first step was to make the mold for her

head. He began to assemble the plastic mold around her skull. He then began to fill it with foam. Once the foam had hardened, he removed the mold and began to clean it up, so that it started to resemble a pure white version of the girl he had hit with his car. He would repeat this with her other body parts. It was a tedious process, but Vincent was nothing if not patient.

As he worked, he couldn't help but imagine what Emily must have been like. She was clearly a kind and caring person and had a bright future ahead of her. He wondered what she would have grown up to be like, had she not died.

Vincent knew she would have become a wonderful person with a strong moral core. She would have done amazing things and changed the world for the better. He knew deep inside, she would still change the world, but not certainly in the way she had thought.

As he continued to work, Vincent felt a strange sensation. It was almost as if he could hear Emily's voice, even if he had never heard it before, whispering to him. It was faint, but he could just make out her words.

"Thank you," she whispered. "Thank you for freeing me."

Vincent looked around, but there was no one there. Still, he couldn't help but smile. It was a beautiful feeling, and he felt as if a weight had been lifted off of his shoulders. He knew that Emily would be grateful for what he had done for her, and that made him happy. After several hours, he had a mannequin in front of him that resembled the fallen nineteen-year-old perfectly.

He had built it out so it looked like the Emily Mannequin was jogging, though her expression was neutral; he would have to work on that for the future. He then began to apply her skin. This was the trickiest part and had to be done with great care. The skin had to be attached perfectly, or else it would look fake.

It was a long and arduous process, but Vincent was patient. He wanted to get it just right and was willing to take the time to do so. He applied her skin slowly and carefully, taking great care to make sure each and every inch was perfect.

He then began the process of coloring and shading her skin. This was the tricky part, as he had to get the colors just right. If he was going to preserve her, he wanted her to look as real as possible.

He worked meticulously, spending hours on each detail. He didn't want her to look fake, or like a bad wax statue. As the hours passed, the sun was beginning to set. Yet, despite the time, Vincent felt like he could continue forever. After all, he had a lot of work to do, and the last thing he wanted was to have a bad result.

The next day, Vincent was greeted by the sight of Emily, the new Emily. She looked like a real woman, and not some mannequin. He couldn't help but admire his handiwork. He had done an amazing job and was proud of his work. He stood back and admired the finished product.

Emily was once again dressed in her running attire, sneakers on her feet, hair in a ponytail. Her cleavage could be seen though her tank top, her now hard nipples pressing against it. Even her belly button was there. She was perfect, and Vincent couldn't help but feel a sense of pride. Too bad he couldn't show her off. Either way though, she will be the centerpiece of his collection.

He took her into the main floor of his house and placed her next to his other work. The others were no match for her. The dogs playing poker looked dull compared to her. Napoleon the pig didn't have the same charm. And Steamboat Willie? Forget about it.

In his own humble opinion, his taxidermy work had never been better. He had done a magnificent job and couldn't be prouder. He knew that Emily would be happy with her new life, and he would continue to care for her and keep her safe. Yes, she was truly a wonderful sight. Vincent smiled to himself and took one last look at the completed Emily. He wanted more. He needed more. Vincent Greenwood, the humble taxidermist was no more. Vincent Greenwood, the serial killer had taken his place.

CHAPTER 2

Escalation

IT HAD BEEN SIX MONTHS since Vincent had accidentally killed Emily Lyon. Since then, he had managed to stay low and avoid suspicion. He had gone through his normal routine, pretending like nothing had happened. However, inside, he was burning with passion. He wanted more, he needed more. He had to find his next subject, and fast. He kept his eyes peeled, looking for anyone that caught his attention. But he was careful, he had to be. If he was caught, it would be all over. So, he watched, and waited, and planned. Eventually, his patience was rewarded, as he came across another potential victim.

She was a young girl, about eighteen years old, with short blonde hair, and a slim, athletic body. Her name was Halie, and she was a student at the local high school. She was a theater and song star and had a lead role in a production of *bye bye birdie*. She was the star of her high school and had many boys drooling over her.

She was a cheerful, energetic girl, who loved to dance and sing. She had a beautiful voice and was a rising star in the musical world. She had a bright future ahead of her, and everyone who knew her adored her. Vincent, however, saw something different. He saw a young woman with the perfect body to preserve, and a voice that would ring through his head forever.

He didn't know much about her, save for her name and occupation, yet he was determined to learn more. For the next month, he low keyed stalked her, using a VPN to look at her social media, following her from a distance, and even getting drone footage of her. He didn't get to close, and kept his distance.

As he watched, he began to learn more about her. Halie was indeed a bright, cheerful, and happy person. She was kind and compassionate, and always helping out her fellow students and friends. She was popular, and was known for her good looks and outgoing personality. Yet, behind her happy facade, was a deeper, darker side. She was lonely. While she had many friends, none of them were really close. They were merely acquaintances, and none of them understood her true feelings.

Halie longed for a true friend, someone who could understand her, and accept her for who she was. She yearned for someone who could truly know her, and appreciate her for who she was. This was a common trend among serial killers, their loneliness was one of their strongest motivators. As Vincent continued to watch Halie, he felt a strange connection with her.

Vincent could see her true self, and understood her. He could see the pain she felt, and the longing she had. He knew that no one else would understand her like he did, and he wanted to change that. He wanted to be her true friend, and show her the love and acceptance she so desperately desired. But how could he approach her?

He couldn't just walk up to her and tell her, "Hi, I'm Vincent. I killed a girl, and I'd like to kill you too." No, he had to be careful, and plan his actions. He had to win her trust, but not get too close lest he become a suspect in her eventual disappearance.

So, he continued to observe her, learning everything he could about her. He learned her schedule, her likes, her dislikes, her friends, and her family. He learned she lived with her parents, both of them being in their forties, and had two siblings, a sister and a brother named Michelle and Daren. He learned about her dreams, her hopes, and her fears. He learned about her passions, and her goals.

He learned that she loved to sing, and dance, and act, even outside of school. He learned that she dreamed of becoming a famous actress, and was already auditioning for various shows. He also learned that she had a boyfriend named Colin, but that they were currently going through a rough patch.

Vincent didn't care about the boyfriend, though he could be useful, as could her siblings. It didn't matter, he would deal with it all, and the end result would be Halie, immortalized.

Eventually, he learned Halie's parents would be out of town soon on a business trip, leaving Halie and her sibling home alone.

This was his chance. Unfortunately for her siblings, they would be caught in crossfire, along with her boyfriend, but he made a perfect scapegoat. Vincent didn't have much time and began to form his plan. He knew what he had to do, and he knew it had to be done quickly and efficiently.

He would kidnap Halie and her siblings and bring them back to his place. He would preserve all three of them. Halie would be the centerpiece, her sister the second, and her brother, the third. They would all be on display together and would be admired when ever he saw them.

Once the parents were gone, Vincent put his plan into action. He followed Halie and her siblings home from school, and saw the boyfriend show up. He didn't care, and didn't pay attention to him, as he was only really focused on Halie. After the four had finished watching a movie together, the boyfriend left, and Halie and her siblings went upstairs to head to bed. Once the lights went out, he moved.

He knew he had to be quick, and didn't have much time. The three had gone to sleep, so they wouldn't hear his approach. Vincent carefully and silently entered the house, and made his way upstairs. He knew where the bedrooms were, and had memorized the layout.

Once he was upstairs, he crept towards Halie's room, and slowly opened the door. Inside, he saw her, lying peacefully in her bed. She was sleeping soundly, and did not stir. He took out a syringe and injected a sedative into Halie's bloodstream. She didn't even react to the pinprick of the needle. He then tied her up and took her to his car. He then returned and did the same with her siblings. He knew that they would
wake up eventually, and he would have to keep them sedated and restrained.

As he drove home, he couldn't help but smile. Everything had gone perfectly, and now he had the subjects for his new project. He couldn't wait to begin his work, and he knew that his art would be more beautiful than ever before. Once home, he carefully carried Halie and her siblings into the basement. He laid them down on the tables and began the process of preparing them for preservation.

He started with Halie, as she was the main attraction. He carefully undressed her, and began to make the necessary measurements. As he worked, he couldn't help but admire her naked body. She was a beautiful young woman, and he was lucky to have her as his subject.

As he continued to work, he began to feel a strange feeling. Vincent wasn't sure what to make of it. He tried to ignore the feeling, but couldn't. It was as if her soul was reaching out to him and was trying to communicate with him. He decided that this wouldn't do and placed a cloth over her mouth and nose. She wasn't conscious, but he could still feel her fighting. He didn't know if it was the drugs, or the thought of death, but she was struggling.

Soon, she was dead. He checked her pulse to be sure, then began to drain her blood. He then opened the girls brown eyes to look into them. They were cold and lifeless, yet somehow, still beautiful. He would miss her eyes, and her soul, but his art came first. She soon was skinned and was on her way to immortality.

Next was her brother, Daren. Vincent had seen Daren at his school from afar. He had a reputation for being a ladies man despite his young age, and had many girlfriends. Vincent didn't care, all he saw was a nice piece of meat. He began by stripping the teen boy, and was surprised at how fit he was. Clearly, Daren was an athlete, and took care of his body. As he began the process of draining the boy's blood, he could not help but feel a sense of excitement. This was his first time working with a male subject, and he was looking forward to the challenge. He was eager to preserve Daren's muscular physique, and was confident that he could do a good job.

Once the blood had been drained, he began to work on the skinning process. This was a delicate task, and had to be done with great care. If anything were to go wrong, the entire project would be ruined. Vincent was meticulous, taking his time and being careful. He wanted to get it right, and he didn't want to ruin the skin. After several hours of careful work, he had successfully skinned Daren's body. He then brought the boy's skin to where he kept his tanning solution, and started to preserve it this way he did before, and then headed back to begin to make a cast of Daren.

Finally, there was the sister, Michelle. She was the middle child and looked like a younger version of Halie, but with longer hair. She was a pretty girl, with a slim, athletic figure. Vincent knew she had a friendly, outgoing personality from his observations, and was well-liked by her peers.

She was a talented musician, and often participated in band competitions and other activities. Now she was to be a taxidermied trophy. Vincent could feel her struggling as he began the process of draining her blood. She was fighting for her life, but he was relentless. Eventually, she succumbed, and her body went limp. He could not help but admire her beauty, even in death. He had chosen his victims well, and would make sure that their sacrifice was not in vain. Their bodies would live on, and their spirits would continue to live through them. They were his, and he would do with them what he wished.

As Vincent began to remove Michelle's skin, he hummed a tune, one that he hummed when working on his animals, this was becoming routine it seems. Once skinned, he brought the layer over to the tanning solution and began the preservation process for the third time that day.

THE NEXT DAY

The sun was shining, and Vincent Greenwood woke up refreshed. It was a new day, and he had a new project. He couldn't wait to get started, and was eager to begin.

He descended into the basement and was greeted by the sight of his new work. The three siblings he had kidnapped the day before were standing there, frozen in time.

Halie, her naked, pale body a stark contrast to her siblings. Daren, his muscles still defined, though slightly less, and Michelle, her hair now a mess. They were beautiful, and Vincent could not wait to begin his work.

He was already planning on a display, and what pose he would use for them. Unlike with Emily, Vincent would be able to pose Halie and her siblings after the fact. For the past six months, he had been working on new designs for their support structure underneath their skin, including being able to change their poses, and in a limited way, their expressions.

Vincent had always had a flair for the dramatic, and his work reflected that. He wanted his exhibits to be beautiful and lifelike, and he always took great care in their creation. He wanted to pose Halie doing what she loved, singing. Her sister would be posed playing her trumpet, and her brother playing the drums so as to match the theme.

He wanted them to be perfect, and he knew that they would be. He was a master at his craft, and he would make sure that his work was the best it could. Vincent soon got to work, manipulating their limbs as he did so. When he was done, the three siblings looked exactly the way he wanted them to look. Halie was in a dress, one that she was fond of wearing, and was poised like a singer. Michelle was in a trumpet player uniform, complete with a hat. Daren was in a band uniform, with drumsticks in his hands.

All in all, Vincent was pleased with the results. They looked lifelike, and he couldn't wait to get them to his trophy room. Once there, he took his time to clean them, and adjusted their poses. Halie's arms were bent, her fingers curled, and her body was facing the audience, or rather, her viewer, Vincent. Her hair was messy, and her glass eyes were staring at the world around her.

Daren's head was down, his arms posed as if moving the drumsticks. His expression was neutral, his body hunched over. His blond hair was in a bowl cut, and his pants were tented.

Michelle was the same pose, but on the other side of her sister, though her expression was more determined. Her lips were puckered, and her arms held a trumpet to it, though no sound would ever come out if it. Her blue eyes were open and staring, while her blonde hair was in a ponytail.

Vincent posed the siblings across from Emily, and knew he had done good work. These three looked perfect, and he was proud of his efforts. The siblings on the other hand did not care in the slightest and couldn't anymore.

As the days passed, Vincent couldn't help but grow more and more attached to his new exhibits. He spent hours each day talking to them, telling them about his day, and sharing his thoughts and feelings with them. He felt a strange connection with them, and he could swear that he could sometimes hear their voices.

He knew it was silly, but he couldn't help himself. He had been alone for so long, and having someone, or rather, something, to talk to was quite a relief. Vincent was also becoming more and more attached to his artwork.

The police had blamed Halie's boyfriend Colin for her and her sibling's disappearance and presumed murder when no bodies were found. He had been arrested not long afterwards and was on trial for murder.

Everyone was convinced he was guilty, to the point that they were having trouble finding an unbiased jury. The community mourned the sibling's loss, but would move on eventually, unless you are Vincent Greenwood.

As for the siblings remaining flesh, he couldn't just throw it out lest someone track him down. So he decided to eat it, coming up with various recipes for human. Was it sick to Vincent, yes, but he deemed it necessary. It wasn't half bad either, with Halie and Michelle being somewhat sweet, while Daren was gamier. He had done the same to Emily when he acquired her. He just couldn't risk disposing of their remains.

Even after reluctantly eating them, Vincent couldn't help but think about his next target. He wanted more, he needed more. Killing it seemed had become an itch that just couldn't be scratched. He would wait for things to calm down, then he would strike again.

CHAPTER 3

Lost Love

A FEW MONTHS HAD PASSED since Vincent had killed Halie and her siblings. Per societal expectations, he had been a good boy so far, but still, he wanted more. More specifically, he wanted someone he admired, but could never have, someone he was denied. He wanted Theresa Johnson wife of the mayor.

Theresa was a beautiful woman, with dark brown hair, and a slim, yet curvy figure. She was the epitome of beauty, and had a kind, gentle soul. She was an advocate for animal rights and was constantly raising money and awareness for various causes. She was an inspiration to many, and her husband was extremely lucky to have her.

Vincent had known her in college, back when she was Theresa Lopez. He always admired her from afar, but could never get the guts to ask her out. Plus, he wasn't good enough for her, or so he told himself. He eventually got professional help for his self-esteem issues, but it seemed to work a bit too well. He now was overly confident and thought he could make her his. As the wife of a public figure, no one would expect him, they would think a radical group first.

Vincent knew he would have to be careful. Theresa was a high-profile target, and if he were caught, he would be in big trouble. But he didn't care. All he cared about was getting his hands on her. Theresa's schedule was public knowledge and always published on the towns website. It was almost as if she wanted someone to take her. Vincent wasn't complaining. He was going to take her, and soon.

One morning, he woke up early and checked her schedule. He saw that she had a meeting at a local animal shelter and would be there all day. It was the perfect opportunity, and he wasted no time. He made sure to pack all the necessary supplies and headed out. The shelter was located on the outskirts of town and was an easy drive.

As he approached, he noticed a small group of protesters, likely from the local extremist church, they seemed to hate everyone, the mayor, his wife, the shelter, Vincent himself even. They were a poor excuse for a church, and perhaps he should pay the leader and their family a visit someday. They had been causing trouble for the town recently and were gaining national news coverage.

Either way, they didn't concern him, he had a job to do. It was cold out today, and Vincent was dressed in a heavy jacket and had a ski mask on his face. Due to the weather, he didn't look out of place. He carefully made his way towards the building, keeping a lookout for any security cameras or guards. He was prepared for any eventuality and would not be caught off guard.

Vincent made his way to the back of the building, where there was a small service entrance. He tried the door, and was pleased to find it unlocked.

He slowly opened the door and slipped inside, being careful not to make any noise. He was greeted by a long hallway, with doors on either side. He listened, and heard the faint sound of voices coming from the end of the hall. He crept towards the voices, being careful not to make a sound.

As he reached the end of the hallway, he peeked around the corner and saw the group of people sitting in a large room, having a discussion. They were engrossed in their conversation, and did not notice Vincent.

Vincent quickly moved behind a large plant,

and waited. He knew he would have to act fast, and he had to be precise.

Suddenly, Theresa stood up and excused herself, saying she needed to use the restroom. Vincent knew this was his chance, and quickly moved from behind the plant. He followed the woman into the restroom, and as she entered a stall, he hit her on the back of the head, knocking her unconscious.

He quickly picked her up and carried her out the bathroom, making his way back down the hallway.

As he made his way towards the exit, he encountered a security guard, who immediately became alarmed at the sight of him carrying a seemingly unconscious woman.

"Hey, stop right there!" the guard yelled. Vincent knew he had no choice.

"Screw you!" He replied and ran.

The guard gave chase, and the two of them raced out the back door, into the cold winter air. Vincent was determined to escape, and quickly put distance between himself and the guard. He could hear the guard calling for backup, but he didn't care. He had his prize, and that was all that mattered.

Vincent raced to his car, and quickly drove away, the tires screeching on the icy pavement. He didn't stop until he was sure he had lost the police. He had done it. Theresa Johnson was his.

Now, the real work could begin.

Vincent had arrived home, with Theresa unconscious in his arms. She was beautiful, even with her hair messed up, and her makeup running. Vincent gently laid her down on the table and began the process of removing her clothes. He had to be careful, as he did not want to damage her body.

Once she was naked, he began the process of preparing her for preservation. He started with her hair, washing and conditioning it until it was soft and silky. He then moved on to her skin, cleaning and exfoliating it until it was smooth and flawless.

He then moved on to her body, massaging it and making sure every inch was relaxed and stress free. Vincent continued with his preparations, making sure Theresa was ready for her new life. He took great care with her, as he knew how special she was. By the time he was done, Theresa was looking perfect, and Vincent was feeling very satisfied. She remained unconscious the entire time, and Vincent would make sure of it, he didn't want to stress her out.

Leaning in, he gave Theresa a kiss on her still lips. He had a few more hours, and decided to get to know her better.

Religious Extremists Kidnap Mayor's Wife

By Jessie Flounder

On Monday, the town was shocked and horrified as extremist kidnappers struck once again. The mayor's wife, Theresa Johnson, has been kidnapped and is presumed to be held hostage.

The incident occurred at the animal shelter on the east side of town. The mayor's wife, while at a meeting with staff had excused herself to go to the restroom. The next person to see her was security guard Ralph Jeeves, who had seen a masked individual carrying Mrs. Johnson's unconscious form out of the shelter and ran when confronted.

Ralph pursued the suspect, but they managed to escape, and get away in a vehicle.

The police have launched a manhunt and are urging the public to come forward with any information they might have.

The mayor and his family are understandably distraught and have asked for privacy during this difficult time.

The town is united in its support of the mayor and his family, and we hope and pray that Theresa will be returned safely.

TWO DAYS LATER

"I'm so glad you're here with me now Theresa", Vincent said, stroking the woman's cheek.

Theresa's brown eyes stared at her secret admirer, not a care in the world. She was now nothing more than an object for Vincent to enjoy, and had been so for the past day. Vincent was enjoying every moment of it.

Her body was completely naked, and was standing at attention, her arms at her sides. Her hair was perfectly styled, and her makeup was expertly applied. She looked like a goddess.

Theresa was his, and no one could take her away from him. No one even suspected him, blaming the extremist group that had been there protesting. They were the ones that had caused a ruckus, and no one would ever know what he did.

He continued to stroke her face, enjoying the feeling of her soft skin against his fingertips. She was his, and he was hers. They were meant to be together, and no one could keep them apart.

"You are so beautiful Theresa," he whispered. "And I am so lucky to have you. We will be together forever, and no one will ever take you away from me."

As he spoke, he could not help but feel a deep connection to the woman in front of him. He felt as if they were kindred spirits, destined to be together.

His love for her was deeper than anything he had ever felt before, and he was certain that it was meant to be. Their relationship was one that transcended time and space, and was stronger than any other.

"I love you, Theresa," he said softly, leaning in to kiss her lips. She did not, and could not respond.

"I will always love you," he continued. Theresa continued to stare at him, her brown eyes blank and unblinking. But Vincent could feel her love for him, and knew that they were meant to be.

Mayor Johnson was utterly distraught. His wife was missing, and no one knew where she was. The police were doing their best, but no leads had turned up.

"How could something like this happen, and to him of all people", he thought to himself. He knew that he was not the most popular person in town, but he did not think that anyone would go so far as to kidnap his wife.

Mayor Johnson was a man who had always put his family first. He still had his daughter Rachel, but she was equally distraught. The media had already dubbed this a political kidnapping, which would not be too far off the mark.

"She's my wife, for Christ sake!" the mayor cried. "They have to find her! They have to!"

He paced around the room, unable to contain his anger and frustration. His wife was the most important thing in his life, and the thought of losing her was too much to bear.

"This can't be happening," he said. "This can't

be happening."

The mayor sat down on the couch and put his head in his hands. This was a nightmare, and he had no idea how he was going to get through it. Suddenly, his phone rang.

"Hello", he said. "What... this this can't be. Not her too!" He dropped the phone on the receiver. His daughter was missing.

Suddenly the Mayor felt a sharp pain in his chest and collapsed to the floor. He was discovered an hour later by his secretary, having suffered from a major heart attack due to shock.

Mayor's Daughter Kidnaped

By Jessie Flounder

Yesterday evening, the town of Pinehurst was once again gripped by horror, as the mayor's daughter, Rachel Johnson was abducted. The mayor was understandably devastated and hospitalized due to shock, and is asking for the public's help in finding his missing wife and daughter.

Rachel is a high school student and is well-liked and well-known in the community.

The mayor has received a lot of support from the community, and the mayor is grateful for everyone's concern and prayers.

He has issued a statement saying that he is confident that Rachel and Theresa will be found safe and sound.

The mayor has asked that anyone with any information please contact the police, as time is of the essence.

In the meantime, the mayor and his family are relying on the strength and support of the community to get through this difficult time.

Vincent Greenwood smiled as he looked upon his latest taxidermy project, that of Rachel Johnson. She was standing there, nude, with her arms outstretched, just like her mother. She had a blank stare on her face, and her dark hair was cascading down her back.

"You're perfect," he said, admiring her stiff form. "Just like your mother."

He had been watching Rachel for a while now, and had seen the sadness and loneliness that she carried with her. He knew that she needed someone who could understand her and accept her for who she was, and he was that someone. She had been an athlete and was an excellent runner. He had seen her at a few meets, and had been impressed by her speed and endurance. She was a true athlete, and was a credit to her sport.

He had taken her while she had been in her school locker room. She had been showering after cross country training, and was all alone. No one had noticed her absence, and no one would miss her, or so he had thought.

The school had immediately closed, and was being investigated, but it wasn't him they suspected. No, it was that was the extremist group, the one that had been blamed for the mayor's wife kidnapping. Their lead pastor been arrested, and would be in jail for a long time.

Meanwhile, the mayor had lost his wife and daughter. The man was distraught, and was doing everything he could to find his loved ones. He had launched a massive search, and was scouring the entire state. However, no trace of the missing women had been found. Rumor was he planned to resign to search for them. Little did he know they were in a cabin a few miles away from him.

The town was in a state of shock and disbelief, and the mayor was a broken man. His family had been ripped from him, and he was struggling to hold on. The media had gone into a frenzy, and was following every lead, no matter how small. Vincent would have to lay low for a while. He didn't care though, he had his prize.

"Rachel, you are mine now," he said, his eyes filled with love and devotion. "I will always be here for you, and I will never let you go."

He placed his hand on her cold cheek, and felt the tears welling up in his eyes. This was the greatest moment of his life, and he was going to savor it.

Vincent knew that he and Rachel would be together forever, and nothing could come between them. He was her protector, her guardian, and her lover. She was his, and he was hers. Forever.

CHAPTER 4

Troupe 1472

TWO YEARS LATER

It had been two years since Vincent Greenwood had kidnapped the Mayor's wife and Daughter, turning them into taxidermied trophies. It had also been two years since Vincent made his last human trophy, a long two years at that. In those two years, he had changed. His confidence had skyrocketed, and he had become much more assertive. He no longer hid in the shadows, but instead, embraced his true self. At least in private he did. He still had an image to maintain, but his new found self confidence did leak through here.

In the two years since he hunted his last human, Vincent art had taken off. He had a dedicated following, and his work was praised by critics and collectors alike. His pieces had been shown all over the country, and his name was becoming known.

Vincent was happy with his life and was content. Still, he missed the thrill of the hunt that he had been developing. On the bright side though, things were starting to calm down. The mayor was out of office and was no longer a threat.

It was the start of a new year, and Vincent was ready to get back to work. He had a new piece in mind, and he was excited to get started. It would be a piece unlike anything he had done before, and he knew it would be his best work yet.

The piece was based on the local Girl Scouts troupe. They were a tight knit group of girls and were always getting up to mischief. Vincent had seen them out and about, selling cookies, and was impressed by their tenacity.

They were a cute bunch, and their youthful innocence was refreshing. He had decided that he would create a piece based on their adventures and show the world just how cute and innocent they were. He would capture their joy, their energy, and their sense of adventure. It would be his most risky piece yet as well.

His first objective was to get close to the Den Mother of the troupe, perhaps start a romantic relationship with her. Luckily, he knew who the den mother was, a woman named Samantha. She was a 30 something young woman, with red hair and freckles. She was energetic and outgoing and was well-liked by everyone.

Vincent had been keeping an eye on her and had noticed that she seemed to be lonely. Maybe he could be the one to make her feel less lonely, and maybe even love her. He was right. As Vincent had anticipated, Samantha was lonely, and was happy to have someone to talk to. They hit it off right away, and soon became close friends.

Samantha was always telling Vincent stories about the scouts, and her adventures with them. She was clearly a dedicated and caring mother figure and was a pleasure to be around. As their relationship grew, Vincent could not help but develop feelings for her. She was sweet, and funny, and always made him laugh.

He found himself wanting to be with her and wanted to get to know her better. Eventually, their relationship evolved into a romantic one, and they were soon dating. But this seemed to complicate things for his plan. How could he turn his own girlfriend into a trophy? It was a conundrum; one he would have to think about.

Meanwhile, Samantha was oblivious to the danger she was in. She was happy to have a boyfriend and was enjoying their relationship.

She was always talking about the scouts, and her plans for their next adventure. She was an inspiration to Vincent, and he could not help but fall more and more in love with her.

He had not been able to tell her the truth about himself, but he knew he would have to, eventually. He knew that the longer he waited, the harder it would be. He had to tell her the truth, and soon.

It was a difficult decision, and Vincent was not sure if he was making the right choice. He knew that once he told Samantha the truth, there would be no going back. Their relationship would be over, and he would lose her. But he knew that he could not lie to her anymore, and that the truth would come out, one way or another. He was ready to tell her and hoped that she would understand.

A few days later, Vincent and Samantha were sitting on the couch, enjoying each other's company. They had been spending a lot of time together and were growing closer by the day.

"Samantha, there's something I need to tell you", Vincent said nervously.

"What is it?", Samatha asked.

"It's about my work."

"Your work? What do you mean? I know you do taxidermy and I already said I'm fine with it."

"I know, and I appreciate that. But there's more to it. There's something you don't know. Something I've been hiding from you."

"What is it?", she repeated, concerned.

"Perhaps it's best if I show you", he said, taking the red head by the hand to his trophy room/showroom. What he did next however was much more of a surprise, he led her to a hidden room. Inside, she saw the former mayor's wife and daughter.

"What is this, Vincent", Samantha asked, her voice trembling. She then spotted three blonde teens in the corner of the room, two of them playing instruments, while the oldest looked like she was singing.

Across from them, there was a brunette who looked like she was jogging.

"Who are these girls?", she asked, her voice barely a whisper.

"They are my trophies. These are all the people I've killed and preserved. I'm so sorry Samantha, I've been lying to you, and I should have told you the truth. If you want to turn me in, I'm not going to stop you. I deserve it."

Vincent braced himself, expecting the worst. Instead, Samantha wrapped her arms around him, pulling him into a tight embrace.

"I forgive you Vincent. I know you're not a bad person", Samantha declared.

"But I've killed people, innocent people."

"You hunted a game animal, an unorthodox one admittedly, but humans are still animals", she said. "You did it fair and square as far as I'm concerned."

"Samantha, you're amazing. I can't believe you're okay with this", he said, still surprised by her response.

"Well, I'll admit, it is a bit... strange. But I can't deny that I love you, and I'll accept every part of you, including this."

She held him close, her face nuzzled against his chest. "I'm just happy that you're finally honest with me, and I can't wait to learn more about you", she said.

Vincent was speechless, he couldn't believe that Samantha was so understanding and accepting. He was so lucky to have her, and he knew that their relationship would only grow stronger from here.

"Did you have any new hunting trips in mind", she asked, raising an eyebrow.

"Uh, I did have an idea for a display with your scouting troupe", Vincent said sheepishly.

Samantha paused and looked up at him. "Are you asking me if you can hunt the Girl Scouts of my troupe, because if you are, I say hell yeah", she said, a wide grin on her face.

Vincent was taken aback, he was not expecting this response.

"You mean, you're okay with me killing and stuffing your Girl Scouts", he asked, still shocked.

"Yeah, I mean, it's kind of creepy, but I love you and I'll support you in anything you do. Plus, it would make a really cool exhibit."

"Thank you, Samantha, you're the best girlfriend a serial killer could ask for", Vincent said, a smile on his face.

A FEW WEEKS LATER

Troupe leader Emma Thomason looked at her fellow scouts as they set up camp. The 14-year-old's dirty blonde hair was in a bun and was currently dressed in her green uniform. Den Mother Samantha had left her in charge while she headed to town to get some supplies they had forgotten.

"Alright everyone, we need to get the tents up before the sun goes down", Emma said. The girls nodded and began working.

As the afternoon progressed, the girls

managed to get the campsite set up, and the tents were pitched. Emma was concerned their Den mother hadn't returned yet, though there could have been traffic. Either way though, they were experienced and knew what they were doing.

Emma was a natural born leader and had been the leader of the troupe for the past year. She was a kind, thoughtful girl, and always put the needs of her troupe first. She was also the oldest, if only by a few days. The other girls were a mix of 13 and 14-year-olds. They were a lively bunch and were always up for adventure. They were also very close and were like sisters to each other.

As the sun began to set, the girls gathered around the campfire, eating s'mores and telling stories. They were having a great time, and were enjoying the feeling of being in nature. Suddenly, Emma heard a sound in the woods. She stood up and called out, "Is anyone there?".

The other girls gathered around her, listening. There was no response, and the girls were getting scared.

"Let's go check it out," Emma said. The other girls nodded and followed her. As they made their way through the woods, the girls were on edge, not knowing what to expect.

Suddenly, a figure appeared in the shadows. It was a man, dressed in black and carrying a rifle. The girls were terrified and started to run. The man chased after them, and the girls scattered, with several of them falling into a pit.

Emma managed to evade the man and was making her way back to camp. As she reached the campsite, she noticed that Samantha had returned.

"Emma, are you okay? I heard the girls screaming", Samantha asked, concerned.

"There's a man in the woods! He's trying to kill us!"

"What?! We have to get out of here!"

Samantha and Emma quickly packed up the tents and supplies, and the two women set off into the night. As they made their way down the trail, Emma noticed that they were being followed.

"Samantha, he's following us!"

"I know, just keep running! We have to get to the road!"

The two women ran as fast as they could, not daring to look back.

As they reached the road, they saw a car approaching.

"Quick, get in the car!" Samantha yelled.

They quickly jumped into the car, and the driver sped away, leaving the man in the dust. As they drove down the road, Emma turned to Samantha.

"Do you know who that was back there?"

"No, I've never seen him before."

"Do you think he was going to hurt us?"

"I don't know, but we're safe now. Don't worry." The two women looked at each other and sighed in relief.

"Ladies", the driver said.

"What", Emma asked. She then turned around, and saw Samantha was holding a syringe. The world went dark.

***

LATER THAT NIGHT

Vincent Greenwood opened the cover off the back of his pickup truck and smiled. He had just come back from a successful hunting trip, and his prey was laying in the back; the twelve girls scouts of troupe 1472. Most were unconscious, though some were dead. It didn't really mater, the same thing was going to happen to them either way.

As he carried them inside one by one, he couldn't help but feel proud of his latest hunt. He had managed to take down an entire scout troupe, and he couldn't wait to begin the preservation process.

The girls were all around 13 or 14 years old, and were in excellent health. He carefully lifted them up, one by one and carried them down to his workshop. His girlfriend Samantha soon arrived in her car and helped him with this, eager to see how he did his magic. Vincent took care to strip and skin each girl, making sure he did not loose track of what belonged to who in life.

Emma Thomson stared ahead lifelessly as she stood in a line up with the rest of her troupe. She and the others had been stuffed and mounted, dressed in their uniforms, and posed in various activities, such as hiking, singing, and even selling cookies. They were posed throughout the secret trophy room. The taxidermist had done an amazing job, and the girls looked as if they were simply frozen in time.

Emma felt nothing as she stood there, her skin now covering a custom-built frame. She was a lifeless husk, a mere shell of her former self. She would remain there, in this room, for all eternity.

Vincent smiled as he looked upon his

masterpiece. It was a tribute to the Girl Scouts, and a reminder of his own prowess as a hunter. He had captured his prey, and was now displaying them for all to see. He turned to Samantha, and they shared a kiss. It was a triumphant moment, and one they would always remember.

"They are perfect", Samantha said.

"Thanks, they were the most challenging group yet", Vincent replied.

"No kidding, it was a little bit of a shock when you showed me the plan and what you were doing to the girls, but I can't deny the end result. This is truly amazing", she said, still a bit shocked at what was before her.

"Well, we do have a lot in common, don't we", Vicent said, winking.

"Yeah, I guess we do", she said, smiling.

"So, what are you planning to do next?", Samantha asked.

"I have no idea. Maybe a group of musicians, or an actress. Who knows?", Vincent said.

"Well, whatever it is, I know it will be amazing", Samantha said. The two looked around the room, admiring the work that had gone into each display. It was truly a testament to the love and skill of a true taxidermist.

"Come on, let's go upstairs and celebrate. You can show me some of your other works, and we can relax.

Vincent and Samantha ascended the stairs, hand in hand. They were happy and content and knew that their love would last forever.

Meanwhile in the darkness of the trophy room, troupe 1472 eyes simply stared forward. No thoughts, no emotions, just emptiness.

CHAPTER 5

Investigation

DETECTIVE SARAH COLLINS maintained her unwavering focus as she continued to probe into the mysterious disappearance of Girl Scout troupe 1472 from their campsite. The den mother Samantha Andrews had reportedly gone to town to pick up supplies, and when she returned, the girls were just gone. She was currently interviewing the woman, as she wasn't beyond suspicion in this disappearance. The room they sat in seemed to absorb the weight of the unanswered questions, its dim lighting casting an atmosphere of suspense and urgency.

"So, can you tell me again exactly what happened?", Sarah asked.

"I told you, I went into town to pick up some supplies we had forgotten, and when I got back, the girls were gone", Samantha told the detective, the annoyance clear on her voice.

"And you have no idea where they might have gone?"

"No, they were just gone. One second, they were there, the next they weren't. I searched everywhere for them, but I couldn't find a trace. It was like they vanished into thin air."

Sarah took a deep breath, trying to stay calm. She knew the woman was telling the truth, but she couldn't help but feel that there was something she wasn't saying.

"And you didn't see or hear anything unusual while you were gone?", she asked.

"Nothing. Everything was quiet. I'm sorry, I wish I could help more, but I just don't know what else to say."

Sarah sat back in her chair, letting out a sigh. She had been on this case for weeks now, and had come no closer to finding any answers. She knew the clock was ticking, and that the chances of finding the girls alive were growing slimmer by the day.

"Thank you for your time, Ms. Andrews. I'll be in touch if I have any more questions", Sarah said, standing up.

"Please, just call me Samantha. And please, if you find anything, let me know. Those girls are like my family, and I can't bare the thought of something happening to them", the den mother said, her eyes welling up with tears.

"I will. We're going to find them, Samantha, I promise", Detective Collins said, patting the distraught woman on the shoulder. She knew deep down that the hope of finding those girls was slim at this point. Perhaps she should return to the scene, see if there was anything she missed. She also still needed to interview the parents of the twelve girls, they having been too distraught to do so until now.

It was a long and arduous drive to the campsite where the troupe had last been seen, the silence in the car deafening. Her partner, Officer Ryan Smith, was driving, his usual joking manner subdued. He hated missing children's cases, even if they were technically teenagers. They almost never ended well.

"This is the place", he said as he pulled into the small parking lot. The campsite was located deep in the woods and would have to hike to the actual site. The area was secluded, with only a few cabins dotted around the area.

"Let's get going. I want to get a good look around before it gets dark", Sarah said, stepping out of the car.

They hiked up a steep hill, and finally reached the top. The view was breathtaking, with the mountains looming in the distance, and the forest sprawling below.

"This place is beautiful", Sarah said.

"Yeah, it's a shame it's tainted by the disappearance of 12 kids", Ryan replied, his tone grim. The two continued on, making their way down to the campsite.

The first thing Sarah noticed was the lack of any
evidence. If there had been any struggle, it was completely cleaned up.

"There's nothing here", she said, her frustration evident.

"Maybe they just left. I mean, it wouldn't be the first time a bunch of kids ran away from their leaders", Ryan suggested.

"Maybe. But they would have come back by now, right", Sarah stated

"Not necessarily. Sometimes they don't want to get in trouble, and will hide for a while", he explained.

"So, what, we just wait around for them to come back? That could take months!"

"I know. But it's the only lead we have right now."

The two sat down, staring at the empty campsite. The wind whistled through the trees, a somber melody that was a fitting soundtrack to their situation.

"Let's start looking around the woods, maybe we can find something they left behind", Sarah said.

The pair made their way through the forest, searching for any clues. They walked for what seemed like hours, the only sounds the rustling of leaves and the chirping of birds. Suddenly, Ryan stopped, holding up a hand.

"Did you hear that?", he asked.

"What? I didn't hear anything", Sarah said.

Ryan motioned for her to be quiet, and the two stood in silence. After a few moments, the sound of footsteps could be heard.

"Stay here, I'll check it out", Ryan whispered, making his way towards the source of the noise.

Sarah stayed where she was, her heart racing. There was a loud crash as the man suddenly fell into the ground. Sarah ran towards the noise, her gun drawn.

"Ryan!", she called out. As she got closer, she saw the man lying on a net in a deep hole.

"Jesus, are you okay?", she asked, helping the man up out of the hole.

"Yeah, I'm fine. But this is weird. This is a bear trap", he said, examining the net.

"Bear traps? In the middle of the woods?", Sarah questioned.

"Well, it would make sense if someone was poaching, but I doubt they're doing that out here", Ryan replied.

"Hmmmm", Sarah said, "I do wonder, and we didn't catch this before."

"What exactly are you implying", Ryan asked, eyebrows raised. The two looked at each other, a realization dawning on them.

"What if this is the reason the girls are missing? What if they fell into a trap like this, and someone took them", Sarah said, her voice trembling.

Ryan's eyes were wide at the realization. "Jesus", he said, the only thing he could say.

"We need to search these woods, now", Sarah said, her voice filled with urgency.

The two began to search the woods, their hearts pounding. As they searched, they came across several more bear traps, each one empty.

"Why would someone go through the trouble of setting up a bunch of traps like this", Ryan asked.

"I have no idea, but it can't be for a good reason", Sarah replied.

As they continued their search, the sun began to set, casting an eerie glow over the forest.

"It's getting dark. We should head back", Ryan said.

"Yeah, I think you're right", Sarah agreed.

The two began their trek back to the campsite, their minds racing with thoughts about the girls, and what could have happened to them.

"You know, this is going to make things much more complicated. If it is a poacher, that means they could be anywhere by now, and we have no idea who they are. Plus, it makes them extremely dangerous", Ryan said.

"We have to keep searching. There has to be something we can use to find these girls", Sarah said, determination in her voice.

As they arrived back at the campsite, Ryan turned to Sarah. "I'll see if the chief can get us a few more officers. We're going to need all the help we can get", he said.

"Good idea. Let's just hope they haven't been hurt", Sarah replied.

They knew they were running out of time, and that every second counted. As the stars began to appear in the sky, they could only hope and pray that the girls were still alive.

"You know, you have a lot of nerve coming here again", the Chief said, his voice full of anger.

"I'm sorry sir, but we have a lead", Detective Collins replied.

"A lead? And what exactly is that?"

"There are traps all throughout the woods. Traps that have caught animals. Traps that have not been reported by the owners of the property."

The chief raised his eyebrows at that. "What kind of traps are they", he asked.

"Bear traps", she replied.

The chief sat back in his chair, taking in the information. "So, your evidence is bear traps, in the woods, where we know there are bears? Sounds flimsy to me."

"We think someone could have used them to catch the girls", Sarah stated.

"So, you're saying that someone set up a bunch of bear traps, and just hoped that the girls would fall into them?", the chief asked.

"Well, no. But it's possible that they were lured into them", Sarah replied.

The chief sighed. "You do realize how this sounds, right? You're accusing a poacher of kidnapping 12 children."

"It's the only lead we have right now, sir", Sarah said, her voice full of confidence.

The chief pinched the bridge of his nose. "Fine, you can look into it. But I'm putting a time limit on this. If you can't find anything in a week, we're pulling the plug on this."

Sarah nodded, anger in the back of her mind at this declaration. "Yes, sir." With that, the chief dismissed the two, and they made their way back to the station.

"So, what's our next move?", Ryan asked.

"We should probably interview the parents", Sarah replied.

"Do you really think they'll know anything? It's not like they were with the girls when they went missing."

"They might have seen something. Even if it was just a weird person around the area. Something is better than nothing at this point." The two sat in silence for a moment, lost in thought. "We have a week. Let's not waste any time."

With that, the two got back to work, determined to find the girls, and bring the person responsible to justice.

Detective Sarah Collins sat in the Thomsons' living room, the weight of their grief palpable in the air. As they recounted the day of the camping trip, Sarah couldn't help but empathize with the parents, their desperation for answers echoing in every word.

"I can't imagine the pain you're going through," Sarah said, her voice filled with genuine compassion. "I want you to know that we're doing everything in our power to find

Emma and the other girls."

Mr. Thomson nodded, his eyes welling with tears. "We just want our daughter back, Detective. We want to know she's safe."

Sarah took a moment to compose herself before delving into the difficult questions. "Did Emma have any friends in the troupe who might have noticed anything unusual? Anything out of the ordinary before the camping trip?"

Mrs. Thomson shook her head, her voice cracking as she spoke. "Emma didn't have a lot of close friends, Detective. She was a quiet girl, kept to herself most of the time." Mrs. Thomson paused, her eyes searching her memory. "Emma was friends with a girl named Lily. They were inseparable, she was one of the other scouts. But no, she never mentioned anything strange. They were just excited about the camping trip, talking about it for days."

Sarah took notes, determined to leave no stone unturned. "Mr. Thomson, can you tell me more about Samantha, the den mother? Did Emma ever mention her being suspicious or acting strangely?"

Mr. Thomson's jaw clenched, his anger barely concealed. "Samantha is a lovely woman. She loves those girls like her own. There's no way she had anything to do with this."

Sarah's eyes narrowed, her suspicions rising.

"I'm not accusing anyone, Mr. Thomson. I'm just trying to get all the facts."

Mrs. Thomson put her hand on her husband's shoulder, her eyes pleading with Sarah. "Please, Detective. Samantha would never hurt those girls. She's a good person. Whatever happened to them, it wasn't her fault."

Sarah nodded, her face softening. "I understand. I just have to look at every possibility, no matter how unlikely."

Mr. Thomson sighed, his body sagging under the weight of his sorrow. "Please, Detective. Just bring our daughter back to us.

Sarah stood up, her resolve steeled. "I promise you, Mr. and Mrs. Thomson. I won't rest until I find Emma and the others."

As Sarah made her way to the door, she couldn't help but wonder if her words would prove to be a lie if the chief shut down their investigation.

"Justice has to be served, and if not, I have to bring some closure to these families. One way or another."

The following morning, Sarah sat in her car, reviewing her notes from the previous day. The interview with the Thomson's had revealed little, but had reinforced her belief that Samantha was involved in the disappearance. She needed to talk to the woman again, to see what she knew.

As she drove towards the den mother's house, Sarah couldn't help but think of the other parents, their faces etched into her mind. Each one had the same look of fear and desperation, the same unspoken question: Where are my daughters?

"We're going to find them," Sarah said aloud, her knuckles white on the steering wheel. "We have to."

She arrived at Samantha's house and was surprised to find an attached shop named Greenwood taxidermy. "Where had she heard that name before", she wondered.

As she stepped out of the car, Sarah took a deep breath, steeling herself for the conversation ahead. She had to stay calm and had to maintain her composure. She could not let Samantha know that she suspected her of having any involvement in the disappearance.

"Here goes nothing," she said, walking towards the front door.

Samantha answered the door and seemed surprised to see the detective. "Detective, what are you doing here?"

"I have a few more questions, Ms. Andrews, if

you don't mind. It won't take long."

Samantha nodded and stepped aside, letting Sarah into the house. As they sat down in the living room, Samantha seemed nervous, her eyes darting around the room.

"Is something wrong, Ms. Andrews?"

"No, I'm just a bit surprised to see you is all."

Sarah leaned forward; her voice low. "Ms. Andrews, I need to know. Do you have any idea what happened to the girls?"

Samantha's eyes widened, her body tensing.

"No! No, I don't have any idea. I've told you, I went into town, and when I came back, they were gone."

"Ms. Andrews, the traps in the woods. Do you know anything about them?"

Samantha looked confused. "Traps? What traps?"

"There are bear traps in the woods, near the campsite."

"Bear traps? Well, I imagine they would be there to catch bears."

Sarah pursed her lips, frustration building inside her. "Ms. Andrews, I know you're hiding something. You need to tell me the truth."

"I'm not hiding anything, Detective. I don't know anything about the traps."

"Fine," Sarah said, standing up. "I'll just have to keep digging." She walked towards the door, Samantha following close behind.

"Please, Detective. Find those girls."

"I will," Sarah said, her voice filled with determination. "I won't stop until I do." As she drove away, Sarah couldn't help but feel like she was missing something.

CHAPTER 6

Trouble Ahead

SAMANTHA ANDREWS TOOK a deep breath as she watched the detective pull away, and waited until the car was over the horizon before moving from her spot. She walked back into the house, her mind racing. She had been lying, of course. She knew exactly what happened to the girls, and why. She just had to wait for Vincent. He was due home any minute now.

Samantha made her way to the showroom for the attached taxidermy shop, and looks over her shoulder to see if anyone was there. She then quickly opens the hidden door in the bookcase, and descends down the steps. The sight is still shocking, despite her having seen it many times. On display were the mounted forms of the 12 scouts, posed in their scout uniforms. She could tell Vincent did his work, each one posed so realistically, the details amazing.

Samantha walks up to one of the girls, a blonde named Lily. She was posed to be standing, holding a box of cookies in her hands as if trying to sell them. Her mouth was open as if yelling to get someone's attention. Her best friend Emma Thompson stood next to her, doing the same thing.

"I'm sorry, girls. I wish there was more I could do. But at least you'll always be here, forever preserved", she says, gently stroking the girl's cheek.

She then walks over to the brunette named Emily. She was posed in a sitting position, a book in her lap.

"You were always the smartest girl, Emily. You could have done anything, been anyone. But now you'll be here, a part of the collection."

She then walks over to the second oldest of the group, a girl named Alex. She was posing as if running, a determined look on her face.

"Oh, Alex. You were always the most active. Always full of energy. But now you'll be here, frozen forever."

Samantha continues her trek, making her way through the rows of girls, pausing in front of each one. "Emma. Lily. Emily. Alex. Allison. Grace. Olivia. Chloe. Madison. Mia. Sophia. Ava. My little angels."

She closes her eyes, imagining the girls

running and laughing, their faces full of life and joy. She couldn't imagine not being with them when they got old enough. They has been her entire life outside of Vincent. She opens her eyes and takes one last look at the girls, a sad smile on her face.

"Goodbye, girls. I love you." She then turns and leaves the room, making her way back up the stairs and shutting the door. As she makes her way back into the house, she hears the front door open.

"Samantha? You home?", she hears Vincent's voice call out.

Samantha hears him coming and puts on her usual demeanor, smiling as he enters the room.

"Hey honey, how was your trip? Did you catch anything good?", she asks, giving him a kiss. Vincent smiles, his face flushed with excitement.

"Oh, it was amazing! I sold a bunch of trophies, my normal ones anyway. Didn't get any of our 'special' game though."

Samantha laughs, glad to see her boyfriend so happy. "Well, that's good. I'm glad you had a good time. I did miss you though." Samantha said, warping her arms around Vincent.

"I missed you too. Anything happen while I was away?"

Samantha tenses slightly, wondering if he knows about the detective.

"Nothing much, just a detective showed up asking about the missing girls. I just told her the same thing, that they were there one moment, and then were gone."

Vincent nodded, his face a mask of concern. "She didn't seem to believe you?"

"No, she was quite persistent. But I'm sure she'll give up soon. It's been several weeks and that police department leaks info like you wouldn't believe it."

Vincent sighed, running a hand through his hair. "I'm worried, Samantha. If the cops start poking around too much, they might find something."

Samantha smiled, placing a reassuring hand on his shoulder. "Don't worry, Vincent. We've been careful. They won't find anything."

Vincent nodded, still not fully convinced. Still, he put on a brave face. "You're right, we'll be fine."

Samantha pulled him into a hug, resting her head on his shoulder. "Everything's going to be fine. I promise."

"Thanks, honey." Vincent held Samantha tight, and for a brief moment, all was right in the world.

The next few weeks were a whirlwind of activity, as the two prepared for their upcoming exhibit. They would be displaying their favorite pieces, and it would be a chance for Vincent to show off his skills to the world.

Samantha had just finished cleaning the display cases when the first guests began to arrive. They were all people Vincent knew from his hunting and taxidermy circles and were eager to see the exhibit.

"Wow, this is some of your best work yet," one man said, his eyes wide as he looked at the mounted animals.

"Thank you, sir. It's been a lot of fun."

Samantha watched from the corner, proud of her boyfriend. She saw him chatting with some other men, and could see the pride and joy in his face. He was doing what he loved, and it showed.

As the evening wore on, and the crowd began to thin, Vincent and Samantha were finally able to enjoy a quiet moment together.

"You did great, babe. The exhibit was a huge success," Samantha said, taking his hand.

Vincent laughed. "Yes, it was a great success he stated. But there is one thing that would make it even better." Suddenly, Vincent got down on one knee.

"Vincent", Samantha gasps.

"Samantha, I know we've only known each other for a short time, but I feel like we've been together forever. You are the love of my life, and I can't imagine my life without you. Will you marry me?"

Samantha stared at him in disbelief, her heart pounding. "Vincent... of course I'll marry you!"

Vincent jumped up and pulled her into a passionate kiss, tears streaming down their faces.

"I love you, Samantha. Forever and always."

The two embraced, the rest of the world falling away. For that moment, it was just them, and their love. And the secret they shared, a secret only they knew.

The wedding was held not long after. It was a small affair, with only a few close friends and family members attending. But to Samantha, it was the happiest day of her life. She couldn't believe she had found a man like Vincent, and that he wanted to spend the rest of his life with her.

As the ceremony concluded and the newlyweds walked out, Samantha couldn't help but smile. She was married to the man of her dreams, and they had a life full of adventure and excitement ahead of them. They soon departed on a honeymoon, no thoughts of human hunting on their minds.

However, for detective Sarah Collin's, things were not all right at all. The case had officially been dropped, and she was told not to investigate further. She wasn't one to let things go, and she was determined to get to the bottom of it. Even if she had to do it on her own time. She still suspected Samantha Greenwood née Andrews, and she was going to prove it.

CHAPTER 7

Inquires

SARAH COLLINS RETURNED to her apartment dejected. Another day, another dead end. It had been a month since the case against the missing Girl Scouts had been dropped, and she had found nothing to support her suspicions. The evidence against the den mother, Samantha Andrews, was circumstantial at best, and the higher-ups were more interested in a quick and easy solution.

"It's not right," she muttered, tossing her coat on a chair. "Those girls are out there somewhere, and no one's doing anything about it."

Sarah just couldn't understand why the police chief was so against pursuing this investigation, the public pressure had to be immense for an answer. She had gone through the paperwork and saw that the families of the missing girls had filed numerous complaints and reports about the police not investigating.

"I just have to find something," she said, pacing the room. "I have to." As she made her way towards the kitchen, her phone buzzed. It was a text from her teen daughter Ann.

"Mom, can you pick me up after school today?" Sarah sighed, her frustration mounting.

"Sure, sweetie. I'll be there," she texted back.

"Thanks! Love you!"

Sarah threw her phone on the counter, her anger threatening to boil over. She knew she shouldn't take it out on her daughter, but she was at her wits' end.

"Why does no one care about these girls? Why is no one doing anything?"

She grabbed a glass from the cupboard, her hands trembling. As she reached for the bottle of whiskey, she hesitated. "No," she said, closing the cupboard door. "I need to stay focused. I can't give up. I won't."

She made her way back into the living room, determination etched on her face. "I'm going to find those girls. And I'm going to bring the person responsible to justice. No matter what it takes."

The sun was starting to set as Sarah pulled into the school parking lot. The sky was awash with beautiful colors, a stark contrast to the storm of emotions rolling inside her. As she stepped out of the car, she saw her daughter running towards her.

"Hey mom, you're a bit late", Ann said annoyed, a hint of sarcasm in her voice.

"You get off at school at four right?", Sarah asked.

"1:30 Mom, four was when middle school got out, I could have walked home by now."

Sarah cursed under her breath. How could she forget such a thing? "Oh, honey, I'm sorry. I guess I lost track of time."

Ann sighed, clearly frustrated. "It's okay, Mom. I know you're busy." Sarah pulled her daughter into a hug, trying to make up for her mistake. The teen seemed annoyed at this and tried to break the embrace.

"Come on, Mom. Not in public."

"Sorry, honey," Sarah said, releasing the girl. "You hungry?"

"Starving," Ann said, a smile on her face.

"How does pizza sound?"

"Great!"

Sarah chuckled at the enthusiasm. "All right,

let's go."

The two climbed into the car and headed for the nearest pizza place. The silence was deafening, the tension between the two palpable.

"So, how was your day?", Sarah asked, trying to break the ice.

"Fine, I guess," Ann replied, staring out the window.

"Just fine?"

"Yeah, Mom, it was fine. Nothing special."

Sarah sighed, frustrated. "Come on, Ann. I'm trying here. You can talk to me, you know."

"It's just, it's the anniversary of when Halie and her siblings..."

Her words trailed off, and Sarah felt her heart ache. "I'm sorry, honey. I should have remembered."

"It's okay, Mom. You've been busy."

Sarah gripped the steering wheel, guilt washing over her. "No, it's not okay. I should have been there for you. I'm sorry, Ann."

"It's fine, Mom. Really. Let's just forget about it, okay?"

"Okay", Sarah said, the two now sitting in silence.

Although they were not talking, an idea suddenly came to Sarah regarding Halie and the Girl Scouts. Maybe, just maybe, the two were connected. But she needed to find out more about Halie, and that would mean meeting her mother... or perhaps her convicted killer. The one that was serving life in prison.

The two soon arrived to the pizzeria and quickly placed their order. As they sat down and waited for their food, Sarah's mind was racing. She had to find a way to bring the two cases together, to connect the dots. She just hoped that she wasn't too late. Soon however, the food had arrived.

"You're quiet", Ann noted, taking a bite of her slice.

"Sorry, just thinking about work," Sarah said, trying to cover her tracks.

"The missing Girl Scouts again?"

Sarah nodded, taking a sip of her drink. "I just can't believe the chief just gave up on those girls."

"People do shitty things, mom." Ann said, taking a bite of her pizza.

"Language, young lady," Sarah scolded.

"Oh, come on, Mom", Ann said, rolling her eyes. "Like you don't swear."

Sarah laughed, her anger and frustration temporarily forgotten. "Maybe, but that's no excuse for you. You're too young."

Ann rolled her eyes, a smile on her face. "Whatever you say, Mom. You're the boss."

The two laughed and joked, enjoying each

other's company. Sarah knew deep down it would be the last time they did so without the stress of what she was about to do on her mind. For now, she would enjoy what she had.

On her next day off, Sarah arrived at Pinehurst penitentiary, to talk to Colin Stein, convicted murderer of Halie Barrow and her siblings Michelle and Daren. She knew the boy had been convicted on flimsy evidence, but was found guilty in the court of public opinion. She hoped what she had to say would get him to talk.

As Sarah entered the visitors room, Colin was already there, handcuffed and wearing an orange jumpsuit. He would be here for the rest of his life, unless she could connect these two cases.

"Mr. Stein, thanks for meeting with me," she said, taking a seat across from him.

"Whatever, lady," Colin said, his eyes filled with contempt.

"I want to talk to you about your victims, Halie, Daren, and Michelle Barrow."

"I've already told you all, I didn't kill them. You got the wrong person, but no one will listen to me."

Sarah smiled, knowing the truth, and the boy's innocence. "I know, Colin. That's why I'm here. I'm going to prove your innocence, and get you out of here."

Colin was flabbergasted. "Are you shitting me? Why would you do that?"

"Because you're innocent, and because I think the person who killed the Barrow kids might also be involved with the missing Girl Scouts."

Colin leaned forward, his eyes narrowing. "What missing Girl Scouts?"

Sarah told him the whole story, about the girls being missing for almost two months. Colin listened intently, his expression becoming more and more concerned.

"That's horrible," he said, his voice barely above a whisper.

"I know. And I think the same person might be responsible for both. I just need your help, Colin. I need you to tell me everything you can remember about the day of the murders."

Colin looked down, his jaw clenched. "I don't know what good it'll do. No one's gonna believe me."

Sarah looked Colin directly in the eye, his blue eyes piercing. "I believe you Colin."

He sat there, looking at the detective, the woman that would be his only hope at freedom. He would take the chance.

"Okay," he said. "I'll tell you everything."

Colin took a deep breath, steeling himself for what he was about to say.

"The day the murders happened, I had gone over to Halie's house to study, then watch a movie. Her parents were gone, so we were alone save for her siblings."

"Was there anything out of the ordinary? Anything that seemed strange or unusual?", Sarah asked, her pen poised to write.

"Not that I can think of," Colin said, his eyes closed as he relived the memory. "Wait, scratch that... I remember as I left, I saw a car parked at the end of the road. It had been there when I first got to the house."

"A car? What kind of car?", Sarah asked, her mind racing.

"I can't really remember. It was dark, and I was more focused on getting home. It looked old though, and kind of beat up."

"Did you recognize the car? Was it someone you knew?"

"No, I'd never seen it before. I just thought it was a neighbor or something."

Sarah nodded, noting down the information. "Anything else?"

"Not really," Colin said. "After I left, I just went home and watched TV. Then the next day, the cops showed up, and the rest is history."

Sarah sat back, her mind working overtime.

It wasn't a lot to go on, and defiantly wouldn't restart any actual investigation, but it was something.

"Thanks, Colin. You've been a big help."

"Do you really think you can clear my name?"

"I do," Sarah said, a steely look in her eye.

Sarah needed to talk to someone who might have seen what happened to those girls, maybe get something in the area that matched the vehicle in the Barrows case, even if it was circumstantial at best. She was determined to find some kind of lead.

So, Sarah decided to visit the parents of one of the scouts, Mia Miller, and her family. They lived just outside of the town limits in a rural area. As Sarah drove down the dirt road leading to the Millers' farm, she couldn't help but notice how peaceful it was.

"This would be a great place for a getaway," she thought, her mind racing with possibilities.

As she pulled into the driveway, Sarah couldn't help but notice the quaint little cottage the Millers called home. It was the kind of place you would see in a magazine or movie, and not real life.

"Wow, this place is gorgeous," she thought. As Sarah climbed out of the car, she was greeted by the sight of Mr. Miller tending to a vegetable garden.

"Can I help you?", the man asked, his brow furrowed.

"Hi, I'm Detective Sarah Collins. I was wondering if I could ask you a few questions about your daughter Mia."

The man sighed, wiping the sweat from his brow. "Detective, if you're here about the missing Girl Scouts, I've already talked to the police."

"Yes, but I have some new information," Sarah said, her gaze unwavering. The man's eyes on the other hand widened.

"New information? About what?"

"About a potential witness, and a vehicle that might have been seen the day of the abductions."

The man stood there for a moment, as if considering what to do. "All right, detective. Let's talk."

The two made their way inside the cottage, and Sarah took a seat at the kitchen table.

"Can I get you anything? Water? Tea?", the man offered.

"No, thank you," Sarah said, a smile on her face.

The man then sat down across from her, a

look of concern on his face. "Detective, what is this new information you have?"

Sarah explained to him about Colin, and his testimony. She also told him about the possible car being seen in the area the day of the murders.

"Now that you mention it, when I dropped Mia off at that parking lot, I do remember seeing an old beat-up car that didn't seem to belong to any of the families I knew. But I can't remember much about it."

"Any details you can give me would be helpful," Sarah said.

The man sighed, running a hand through his greying hair. "Let me see. It was a light color, maybe blue or white. And it was definitely old. Probably from the 70's or 80's."

Sarah noted down the information, her mind racing. "Could it have been a station wagon?", she asked.

"Maybe. I'm not really sure. It was pretty beat up though, definitely not in the best shape."

"Okay, Mr. Miller. Thank you for your time," Sarah said, standing up.

"You're welcome, Detective. Please, find my daughter."

"I will," Sarah said, determination in her voice.

As Sarah left the cottage, she felt a sense of hope. She needed to talk to the DMV and see who still had a registered station wagon from the 70s and 80s. She was going to find those girls, even if it was the last thing she ever did.

CHAPTER 8

Eat The Rich

36-YEAR-OLD MEGAN NANCE was an avid hiker, and just loved all things nature. It wasn't too dangerous after all, and her husband owned a large part of the forest around their estate. So, she always went hiking by herself, and had a great time.

Megan's black hair was currently tied in bun, and she was dressed in a pair of jeans, hiking boots, and a purple t-shirt with a vest on. He had a small ruck on her back in case she needed supplies of some sort.

It was a beautiful day, and the sun was shining brightly as Megan made her way along the trail. She had been hiking for a few hours, and was beginning to feel a bit tired.

"Maybe it's time to head back," she thought, glancing at her watch. Just then, Megan heard a rustling sound coming from behind her.

"Hello?", she called out, her voice echoing through the trees. There was
no response, but the rustling grew louder.

"Hello? Is anyone there?", Megan asked, her heart starting to race. Still, no one answered. Megan began to panic, her body tensing as she prepared to flee.

"I'm warning you!" Still nothing, maybe it was an animal?

Megan turned around and started to run back down the trail. As she ran, she heard the sound of footsteps behind her, growing closer and closer.

"Oh, God," Megan thought, her mind racing. "I'm going to die!"

She ran as fast as she could, her lungs burning, her legs aching. She could feel the fear coursing through her veins, her heart pounding in her chest. She was focused on getting out of there as fast as possible, so focused in fact that she failed to notice she went down the wrong trail, and right over a cliff.

With a scream, Megan plummeted into the ravine below, the last thing she saw was the sky and trees. Then darkness.

Vincent Greenwood frowned as he made his way down the ravine where is quarry had fallen. He wasn't happy and was worried Megan would be damaged beyond repair.

The hunter and taxidermist made his way down the steep, rocky slope, his eyes scanning for any signs of life. The sound of running water echoed through the forest, and the air was thick with the smell of pine.

As Vincent got closer to the bottom of the ravine, he began to see the unmistakable shape of a body.

"There you are," he said, his voice barely above a whisper.

He moved carefully, not wanting to fall himself. When he got close enough, Vincent saw that the woman had landed on her side, her arm twisted at an unnatural angle. Her eyes were open, staring into the abyss, and her face was contorted in a grimace of pain.

Vincent reached down and felt for a pulse, but there was none. The woman was dead. She defiantly wasn't suitable for a full body display.

"Damn it", he said kicking a rock. He then looked at the twisted body of the socialite. Her head was still in good shape, he thought to himself. Perhaps her could do a partial mount of just her head.

He smiled to himself. This would be a new

trophy for his collection. A rich socialite, who fell to her death while trying to escape the horrors of the wild. It was almost poetic.

But, first, he had to get the body back to his workshop. And he had to make sure no one would find out what he had done. Vincent set to work, dragging the body back to the main path and his awaiting truck.

He made sure to place the body in the truck bed and covered it so no one would see. He then got in and started for home.

Vincent circled around the body hanging by her feet, upside down in his workshop. He was currently draining said body's blood.

Megan Nance's eyes stared forward, not a care in the world. Vincent chuckled, she really was a perfect specimen. Her dark hair was long and luscious, and her face was smooth and flawless. Her body was fit and toned, with curves in all the right places, albeit dented and bruised. He walked over and placed a hand on her cheek, caressing it gently.

"You're going to make a beautiful trophy," he said, his voice low.

Vincent then walked over to his tools and

selected a knife. He took it to the woman's throat, and began to cut. Blood flowed freely from the wound, coating the ground below. Vincent worked quickly, slicing and dicing with precision.

Soon, he had removed the head, and held it up for inspection. Megan stared at him, her brown eyes vacant, jaw slack. Vincent smiled at this and brought the socialites head to his workbench and set it down before returning to her body, which still hung from the roof. He would have to butcher this, and in a couple of hours, only the head of Megan Nance would remain of her existence.

A few hours later

When it was done, the hunter and taxidermist looked over his work. He was quite proud of the end result. Megan's head was now on a plaque, and was mounted on the wall in his secret trophy room. Her glass eyes stared out, looking upon the other occupants of the room. Her name was etched below it on a gold plaque.

"Well, Megan. Welcome to the collection," he said, chuckling to himself. He took a step back and admired his handiwork. "Yes, a beautiful addition," he said. "Quite beautiful indeed."

With that, the man exited the room, making sure to close and lock the door. He then headed to his kitchen, where a slab of meat sat on the counter. It looked unrecognizable from the animal it came from, that being the behind of Megan Nance. His wife was away at a meeting in the city regarding the missing Girl Scouts. He was on his own for dinner that night. And he was going to eat well.

Detective Sarah Collins was not happy that she had been pulled away from the Girl Scout and Burrows cases, but maintained her focus as she probed into yet another mysterious disappearance, that of socialite Megan Nance. The chief was defiantly far more interested in solving this case than the girls scout one. The room they sat in seemed to absorb the weight of the unanswered questions, its dim lighting casting an atmosphere of suspense and urgency.

"Mr. Nance, we're doing everything in our power to locate Megan," Detective Collins reassured, her gaze steady as she observed the weariness etched on Mark Nance's face. "Now, let's go back to that morning. Did Megan mention any recent changes in her life, any concerns or fears that might have prompted her to go off the grid?"

Mark pondered the question for a moment, trying to recall any subtle shifts in Megan's demeanor. "No, detective, everything was normal. We were planning a weekend getaway, looking forward to some time together. There were no signs that she was troubled or facing any issues."

Detective Collins nodded, her pen poised over the notepad. "And her relationships, both personal and professional. Were there any tensions or conflicts that you were aware of?"

Mark furrowed his brow, contemplating the complexities of Megan's social circles. "Megan was well- liked by everyone. She had a few close friends, and her work at the charity foundation never seemed to involve any conflicts. I can't imagine anyone harboring ill intentions towards her."

Detective Collins made a note of Mark's responses, her mind churning with possibilities. "We understand that Megan enjoyed disconnecting during her hikes. Did she ever mention encountering anything unsettling during her previous outings? Animals, strangers, or anything out of the ordinary?"

Mark hesitated before responding, "Not

really. Megan loved the serenity of the woods. She often said it was her escape. She felt at peace surrounded by nature, and I respected her need for solitude during those times."

The detective leaned forward, her eyes focused and intent. "Mr. Nance, we need to consider all possibilities. Is there anything about Megan's past, perhaps something she didn't share with you, that might help us understand her disappearance?"

Mark sighed, grappling with the complexity of the situation. "I thought I knew everything about her, detective. Megan was an open book. We shared our lives, our dreams. There's nothing hidden that I'm aware of."

Detective Collins nodded, absorbing the information as she continued her thorough investigation. "We will keep searching, Mr. Nance. I promise you, we won't rest until we find Megan. In the meantime, if anything comes to your mind— no matter how insignificant it may seem— please don't hesitate to contact us."

"Thank you, Detective. Please, let me know if there's anything else I can do to help."

"I will, Mr. Nance. Thank you for your time."

Detective Collins stood and extended her hand, her expression sympathetic and resolute. "We will do everything in our power to find Megan. Rest assured; we won't give up."

Mark shook her hand, his face lined with

concern. "Again, thank you, Detective. Please, bring her home safely."

"We'll do our best," Detective Collins replied, her voice calm and confident.

With that, the detective exited the room, her mind racing as she attempted to connect the dots in this puzzling case.

"One mystery at a time," she said to herself. "We'll solve this, and then we'll get back to those girls."

But she knew the truth, the chief wasn't letting her or her partner return to those cases. Ever. They weren't from rich families, Megan Nance was.

As she climbed into her car, the detective glanced at the photos of the missing girl scouts that were pinned to her dashboard, a constant reminder of the mysteries still unsolved.

"Don't worry, girls. We'll find you," she said, determination etched on her face. "I promise."

With that, she started the engine and drove off into the night, ready to face whatever challenges awaited her.

***

LATER THAT NIGHT

The dim light in Mark and Megan Nance's bedroom cast eerie shadows as a grandfather clock struck midnight.

"Megan," the husband cried out. He had been in bed for hours, but couldn't sleep. He just couldn't stop worrying about his missing wife. He reached out and touched her pillow, which still bore the faint scent of her shampoo. He felt a lump forming in his throat, and tears welled in his eyes.

"Megan, where are you? Please, come home," he whispered.

The house was quiet, save for the ticking of the clock and the faint hum of the refrigerator. That is until a window on the first floor is quietly opened.

A hooded figure slowly made their way through the darkened home, their movements quiet and deliberate. They paused briefly, listening for any sounds of activity, before moving toward the stairs. The figure ascended the stairs silently, their boots making no sound on the carpeted steps. A gun with a silencer was in his hands. He knew he would need to work fast and silently.

As the figure approached the bedroom door, the knob slowly turned and the door creaked open.

Mark bolted upright, his heart pounding as he heard the intruder. "Who's there?", he called out, his voice shaky.

There was no answer, just the sound of footsteps approaching the bed. Mark fumbled for the lamp switch, his hands trembling. As the light came on, the figure stood before him, their face hidden beneath a black mask.

"Who the hell are you", Mark yelled out. These would prove to be his last words as a bullet was fired into the man's chest. "Why", he croaked painfully.

"I simply wish to reunite you with you wife", the masked figure said coldly. He then proceeded to fire more rounds, each hitting the man square in the chest. Mark let out a final gurgle as his body slumped over, the life leaving his eyes.

The figure took a moment to admire his work, the blood spatter on the wall and sheets. He checks to make sure the man was dead, and once he is satisfied, he took a knife he had on him and began to cut his throat. Eventually, he twisted the head of Mark Nance away from his body.

The masked man placed the head of Mark Nance in a sack he had been carrying on him and left the house the same way he had come in, without a sound.

Sarah simply could not believe it as she and her partner Ryan pulled up to the crime scene at the Nance manor. Police barricades were set up, and there were dozens of cop cars. The Chief was going all out on this. She thought she knew why.

As they entered the home, Sarah couldn't help but feel a sense of dread. She had never seen anything like this, and the brutality of the scene was chilling.

"My God," Ryan whispered, his face pale.

Sarah walked around the crime scene, taking in the details. Mark Nance was laying on the bed, his body lifeless and bloody. His head was missing. The man she had talked to only a day prior was dead. This couldn't be a coincidence. That also meant that Megan Nance was also likely dead.

"Fuck", Sarah thought to herself. "Fuck." Sarah's mind raced, trying to process the horror that lay before her. Who would do such a thing? And why?

"This is sick," Ryan said, his voice trembling. "We need to find the son of a bitch who did this."

"Yeah, we do," Sarah replied, her expression grim.

As the two detectives left the scene, Sarah couldn't help but think that whoever had done this had something to do with the missing Girl Scouts, and the Burrow siblings, and lots of other cold cases. She was determined to find the truth, no matter what.

Vincent Greenwood was whistling a tune as he hung his latest masterpiece in his hidden trophy room, right next to the head of Megan Nance.

"Ahh, the perfect spot," he said, taking a step back to admire his work.

He had spent the last couple of days skinning and preparing the head of Mark Nance for display.

"It's good to be the king," he thought to himself, a smile playing on his lips. "Keep up the fort girls", Vincent said to the taxidermied Girl Scouts that lined the room. He brushed the hair of a dark-haired girl named Alex. She did not react to this, and only wobbled in place, her pose running somewhat unstable.

With that, the man departed the room, turned off the lights, and closed the door. He wondered who his next target would be. Vincent chuckled to himself, the work of an artist was never complete.

CHAPTER 9

Family Ties

SAMANTHA GREENWOOD sat in her car, watching for some potential prey for her husband. She was currently parked outside a university hospital, waiting to see if a med student caught her fancy.

"This one's pretty cute," Samantha thought, smiling to herself. The young man was tall and muscular, with short brown hair and hazel eyes. He had an easy smile, and a boyish charm about him.

Samantha's eyes followed the man as he made his way across the parking lot, his medical bag in hand. She noticed how his scrubs hugged his body, accentuating his broad shoulders and trim waist.

"Yep, that one's a keeper," she said, chuckling to herself. She then took a picture of the man, and returned to her task, looking for more quarry.

"This one looks pretty, and looks smart too," Samantha thought, eyeing a young woman who was walking briskly across the lot, a stack of textbooks in her arms.

The woman had long blonde hair, and a petite frame. She was dressed in a white lab coat and dark blue scrubs, and looked every bit the intelligent doctor-to-be.

"Yeah, that one will be good too," Samantha said, taking a photo of the woman as well.

Samantha continued her observations, noting down various potential prey, including a male and female nurse, and a male and female resident.

"All right looks like I've got a full roster," she said, a sly smile playing on her lips. "Time to head home and let Vincent take a look."

With that, the woman started her car and pulled out of the parking lot, heading for the highway.

***

11:30 PM

At the police department, Detective Sarah Collins was working late, trying to piece together the clues in the Burrows and the Girl Scout cases. It was proving to be a frustrating task, as the lack of evidence and leads made it difficult to progress.

"Damn it," Sarah said, slamming her fists down on her desk. She was growing more and more frustrated by the day, and this wasn't helped by the fact she had to do this on her own time, lest she 'waste' department resources.

"Come on, there's got to be something here," Sarah said, her eyes scanning the pages of case notes and witness statements.

As the clock ticked closer to midnight, Sarah found herself becoming increasingly discouraged. She decided to call it a night and head home. She would have to get back at this tomorrow. But tomorrow would not be a good day, far from it.

As Sarah entered her home, she was greeted by the sight of her Daughter sleeping on the couch. Sarah smiled at this, Ann always liked the couch better than her bed for some reason. Memories of Ann growing up soon flooded the detective's mind, the joy, the happiness, the sadness, the heartache.

"What would happen if I can't protect her?", Sarah asked herself, a chill running down her spine.

The woman sighed, pushing her morbid thoughts aside. She couldn't dwell on what-ifs and maybes, she had to focus on the present, and doing the best she could.

Sarah carefully placed a kiss on her daughter's forehead and pulled a blanket up on her prone form. She would keep fighting for her. For them.

And with that, the detective headed off to bed, hoping that tomorrow would be a better day.

On a serene and sun-drenched afternoon, Vincent found himself once again navigating the familiar grounds of Pinehurst National Park's visitor center. His sharp, predatory eyes meticulously scanned the surroundings, seeking potential victims like a wolf hunting in plain sight. His focus locked onto a young family joyfully playing near the park's fountain, the parents seemingly unaware of the malevolent presence that lingered nearby. Their carefree laughter and smiles painted a picture of innocence, a stark contrast to the darkness that loomed over them.

Samantha had suggested some Med students for his next hunt, and while he agreed their were all cute and would make a fine addition to the collection, he wasn't completely sold. But this family, they seemed to scratch an itch he had. They were perfect. The family consisted of two parents, a boy and a girl.

The father had brown hair, and brown eyes. He was tall, and athletic. The mother had long blonde hair, and blue eyes. She was a petite woman, but had a nice figure. The boy had the same brown hair and eyes as his father, and was lanky, but would soon grow into his limbs. The girl was blonde like her mother, and had blue eyes. She was small and would probably remain that way.

Vincent watched as the family enjoyed their picnic, oblivious to the danger lurking nearby. He could already imagine the trophies they would make. He needed to have them, then, and only then would he go after the med students.

"Soon," he thought, a wicked grin spreading across his face. "Very soon."

The man and wife, John and Jennifer Gardner, and their two children John Jr. and Anna, had come to the park to have a picnic, and spend some time together.

Jennifer smiled as she watched her children play, their laughter and smiles filling her heart with joy.

"This is what it's all about," she thought, a

contented sigh escaping her lips.

Her husband, John, wrapped his arms around her, pulling her close. "You know, it's times like this when I realize just how lucky I am," he said, his voice low and husky.

Jennifer smiled, her gaze never wavering from her children. "Yeah, me too," she replied, a note of wistfulness in her voice.

"We really are blessed," John said, pressing a kiss to the top of his wife's head.

The pair watched as their children ran and played, their laughter echoing through the air.

"They're so beautiful," Jennifer said, her eyes glistening with tears.

"Yes, they are," John replied, his voice thick with emotion. "They're the best thing that's ever happened to us."

As the sun slowly began to set, casting a warm glow over the park, Jennifer felt a sense of peace and contentment wash over her. Little did they know, this would be the last time they would feel this.

Later that night, the family was tucked away in bed in their home. Jennifer and John slept soundly, unaware of the horrors that were about to befall them. The children were also asleep, dreaming of their future adventures.

But unbeknownst to them, a shadowy figure crept through the house, their movements silent and deliberate.

They first came to the children's room, the door closing behind them silently.

Inside, the figure saw the two sleeping figures, and smiled. This would be an easy hunt, and would bring back many trophies. He took out a syringe filled with a green liquid.

"Sweet dreams, little ones," the figure whispered, injecting the two sleeping children with the liquid.

Within moments, the children's breathing slowed, and their bodies became limp, before ceasing breathing all together. He would come back for them later.

With the children taken care of, the figure made their way to the parent's bedroom. As they opened the door, the moonlight shone through the window, illuminating the sleeping forms of Jennifer and John. Soon they too were injected with the same green liquid as their children, and they soon went limp as well.

"Perfect," Vincent whispered, admiring his work.

He then went back to the children's room and proceeded to take John Jr.'s body down and out of the house to his truck. He the returned for his sister Anna and did the same with her. After the children were taken, the figure went back for the parents.

Vincent chuckled to himself as he loaded John and Jennifer's lifeless bodies into his truck, the weight of his new trophies providing a satisfying sense of accomplishment. He looked at the scene of the happy family's bodies entangled together and chuckled. He was going to have so much fun mounting them, he couldn't wait.

Vincent's workshop lay shrouded in dimness, a solitary bulb flickering overhead and casting eerie shadows that danced upon the peeling walls. The air was thick with the sickening stench of decay, intermingled with the metallic tang of blood that permeated the desolate space. At the center stood a wooden, dusty table, upon which rested the taxidermied bodies of the ill-fated family – father John, Mother Jennifer, and their two children, John Jr. and Anna. Their lifeless faces, adorned with unchanging smiles, reflected a grotesque snapshot of eternal bliss, forever preserved in a sinister display.

Vincent chuckled as he surveyed his gruesome handiwork. He had spent hours meticulously flaying the skin from the family's bodies, preserving each layer with a mixture of chemicals and preserving agents. The process had been painstakingly arduous, yet his craftsmanship was impeccable. As the lone lightbulb flickered, the shadows seemed to dance upon the macabre scene, giving the illusion that the family was still alive.

"Good evening, my dear friends," Vincent greeted them, his voice a calm and bone-chilling echo in the stagnant air. "I trust you're all doing well tonight?" Of course, there was no reply from the lifeless forms, yet Vincent derived a peculiar solace from their silent presence. In his distorted reality, he believed their stillness signified a continuation of their existence, acknowledging the power and control he had wrested over their lives.

Vincent, the architect of this macabre scene, ran his fingers tenderly over little Anna's cold cheek, a twisted grin contorting his lips. She did not respond, as she was nothing more than a trophy. The same could be said for her brother and parents.

"I hope you're enjoying your new home," he mused, a dark chuckle escaping his lips. "It's the least I could do, after all you've done for me. Your sacrifice is appreciated, I assure you."

Vincent's words were met with silence, save for the faint scratching sounds of vermin scurrying about in the darkest corners of the room. He paid the scavengers no mind, his attention focused solely on the family's preserved remains. Moving with a calculated purpose, he approached John Jr., crouching down to meet the emptiness within the boy's gaze. Vincent's fingers ran through the matted texture of the boy's hair, savoring the tangible remnants of his malevolence.

"Ah, John Jr.," Vincent said, a sinister grin etched upon his face. "The pride and joy of your family, or so I've heard. The apple of your parents' eyes, and the lifeblood of your little sister."

The man's words dripped with a vile venom, yet he remained unfazed, continuing his diatribe in a tone that was equal parts mocking and reverent.

"I must say, you turned out beautifully, my boy. Your skin, so soft and supple. And those eyes, the windows to your soul. So full of life, so full of wonder and promise. A shame, really, that all of that was taken from you."

Vincent's fingertips grazed the child's lifeless eyes, relishing the momentary contact. He then traced a path down the boy's cheeks, jawline, and neck, stopping at the hollowed-out cavity where his heart had once been.

"Yes, you've given me quite a lot to work with, John Jr.," Vincent stated, a note of admiration lacing his words. "A true artist's canvas, if there ever was one."

The man continued his macabre

examination, his hands exploring every inch of the child's body. His touch was methodical, yet tinged with a strange sense of intimacy, as if the boy was still alive and breathing beneath his fingertips.

"And your father, oh your father," Vincent said, moving on to the lifeless form of John Gardner Sr.

"Strong, proud, and protective. Yes, you were his greatest accomplishment. I can see it in his eyes, the way he looks at you. You were his reason for living, and now you are mine."

Vincent's fingers gently caressed the man's skin, admiring the intricate details of his muscular form. He then moved to the man's eyes, tracing the delicate lines around the irises.

"Yes, John. You've done well. I can tell you lived a good life. It was a pleasure taking it from you, truly."

Vincent's gaze then shifted to the woman, the matriarch of the family. Her face, once full of love and warmth, was now devoid of emotion, frozen in a state of perpetual tranquility.

"And you, my dear Jennifer. Mother of two, wife to John. The glue that held this family together."

Vincent's fingers roamed across her features, noting the subtle shifts and curves of her facial structure. He then moved lower, his touch exploring her bare torso, lingering on her supple breasts.

"Yes, Jennifer. You were a special one. So caring, so selfless. A true inspiration, if I may say so myself."

The man's words were met with a resounding silence, yet he seemed unfazed, his voice steady and confident. He was in complete control, reveling in the power and authority he had over the lifeless bodies.

"Well, I must say, it's been a pleasure getting to know you all," Vincent said, a twisted smile forming on his lips. "But, as they say, all good things must come to an end. Don't worry, though. You'll get to meet your friends in the trophy room soon."

With that, Vincent retreated into the darkness, leaving the family to rest in solitude.

Detective Sarah Collins was getting desperate and annoyed at the same time. Another disappearance, this time an entire family, up and vanishing into thin air.

"This can't be a coincidence," Sarah muttered, pacing back and forth in the police station's conference room.

"No shit, Sherlock," Detective Ryan Smith quipped, his gaze fixed on the whiteboard.

Sarah shot him a glare, her eyes narrowed. "What the hell is wrong with you, Ryan? People are going missing, and all you can do is make jokes? This is serious."

"Lighten up, Sarah," Ryan replied, a smirk on his face. "It's not the end of the world."

Sarah threw her hands up in exasperation. "Are you fucking kidding me, Ryan? People are dying, and all you can think about is yourself?"

Ryan rolled his eyes, unfazed by Sarah's frustration. "Look, we don't know if they are dead or not", Ryan said trying to defend himself.

"You know how missing person cases work, especially when they involve children." Sarah said this with a fury in voice that she had never experienced before, so much it silenced her partner.

"I just..." Ryan began. "I just don't see what the big deal is. It's not like we're dealing with the Ripper here."

"Are you really comparing this to Jack the Ripper, Ryan?" Sarah asked incredulously. "This is a serial killer. A sick fuck who's targeting families and abducting them."

Ryan shrugged, a nonchalant expression on his face. "So, what if they're dead? They're not the first people to die, and they won't be the last."

Sarah felt her anger rising, a surge of red hot rage coursing through her veins. "How can you be so callous, Ryan? These are people's lives we're talking about. They have families, friends, people who care about them."

Ryan let out a snort, shaking his head in disbelief. "They're not the only ones, you know. We have a job to do, and it doesn't include worrying about every Tom, Dick, and Harry who go missing."

"You're such an asshole, Ryan. You know that?" Sarah spat out, her hands clenched into fists. She then stormed out of the room so as to not lose her cool and take out her anger on him. The woman then walked to the chief's office and knocked.

"Come in," came the deep baritone of the man, his voice gruff and authoritative.

"Chief, we need to talk about this case," Sarah said, stepping into the room.

The chief sighed, rubbing his temples. "What is it, Collins?"

"Sir, these disappearances are connected. I can feel it in my bones. There's a serial killer on the loose, and we need to do something about it."

The chief looked up, his eyes filled with weariness. "Collins, I know you're trying to do the right thing, but we have no evidence.

No bodies, no witnesses, no leads. We don't know if there really is a serial killer, it's all circumstantial. I'm not willing to invest department resources on such frivolities."

"With all due respect, sir, the missing families aren't a 'frivolity'," Sarah said, her tone defiant. "They're people with lives and loved ones, and they deserve justice."

The chief pinched the bridge of his nose, his frustration evident. "Collins, I understand you're passionate about this case, but we need more to go on. Until then, we can't do anything."

"So what, we just wait for more people to go missing? That's not good enough, Chief!" Sarah exclaimed, her voice rising in pitch.

"We can't act without evidence Collins. If you're not able to follow protocol, then maybe you're not the right person for this job," the chief said, his words laced with a subtle threat.

Sarah stood there, stunned and enraged. "Is that a threat, Chief ?" she asked, her voice trembling.

"Consider it a warning," the chief replied, his gaze cold and unwavering. "Now, get back to work. And keep your head on straight, Collins. We can't afford to have anyone lose focus."

With that, the chief turned his attention back to his paperwork, dismissing Sarah from his office.

Sarah stood there for a moment, seething. The chief was against her, her own partner was now against her, what had happened here? She simply didn't understand. The only one who seemed to be on her side was herself.

She had a bad feeling that if she didn't find the truth soon, more families would disappear, and perhaps even be murdered. She had to figure out what was happening. And she needed to figure it out soon.

CHAPTER 10

Break In

IT WAS OFFICER RYAN Smith's day off, and he decided it would be best to spend some time with family, as this always a good thing to do. Something he noted that his partner Sarah Colins often failed to take time to do herself. "Her daughter really deserved better", he thought to himself as he pulled up to a popular BBQ restaurant named the Pine Grill.

Exiting his vehicle, he quickly heads inside and scans the table for his half sister. He soon finds her sitting with her new husband at a booth in the corner of the restaurant.

"Hey Samantha", he called out with a smile.

Samantha Greenwood turned around, and smiled back at her brother. "Ryan! It's so good to see you," she said, rising from her seat and embracing him.

"Yeah, it's been a while," Ryan replied, his

tone slightly apologetic. "Vincent", he said, acknowledging his brother-in-law.

"Ryan", the man replied.

"So, what have you been up to? How's work going?", Samantha asked, her voice filled with genuine interest.

Ryan chuckled, shaking his head. "You wouldn't believe the cases we've been dealing with lately," he said, his expression becoming serious. "I do worry about my partner sometimes though."

"Oh? What's going on?", Samantha asked, her curiosity piqued.

"It's the strangest thing," Ryan replied, lowering his voice. "People are disappearing, and we have no idea where they went."

"O.K, that seems like the definition of a missing persons case, is it not", Samantha asked sarcastically. Ryan simply glared at his half-sister.

"What, that's not weird enough for you?", he said, rolling his eyes.

Samantha chuckled, shaking her head. "It's definitely weird, but if you remember, I had an entire Girl Scout troupe disappear on me", Samantha said sternly.

Ryan winced at this, having forgotten. "Sorry. Didn't mean to offend, or bring back memories of that. I know it hurt you. I guess the stress is just getting to me, and I'm not thinking straight."

"It's okay, Ryan. You were saying about your partner?"

"Yeah. Sarah Collins. She's convinced there's a serial killer on the loose, but the chief's not buying it. We don't have any evidence to back up her claims, and it's starting to put a strain on our partnership."

"Oh her", Samantha said annoyed. "She's the one who keeps coming by our place about the girls. I keep telling her the same things. It just... it gets stressful."

"I'm sorry, Samantha," Ryan said, reaching out and placing a comforting hand on his sister's shoulder. "I can talk to her, if you'd like. Maybe I can get her to ease up on the investigation. At least when it comes to you."

Samantha nodded, a sad smile playing on her lips. "Thank you, Ryan. I appreciate that. You're a good brother, you know that?"

"I try," Ryan replied, grinning. "But enough about me. How are things with you two besides the obvious."

"Oh, they're good. Vincent's been a bit stressed with work lately, but other than that, everything's great," Samantha said, smiling at her husband.

"I'm glad to hear that," Ryan replied, genuinely happy for his sister. "Any plans to uhh... get me a niece or nephew?

Samantha laughed, shaking her head. "Well, we're certainly trying. And if you're lucky, you might get your wish sooner than later," she said, her smile widening. Ryan's eyes widened, while Vincent looked on dumbfounded.

"Wait what?", Vincent asked surprised.

"I'm pregnant, Vincent," Samantha announced, her voice filled with excitement. She then wrapped her arms around her husbands neck and kissed him on the nose.

"Oh my God, Samantha, that's incredible! Congratulations," Ryan exclaimed, hugging his sister.

Vincent was shocked. He didn't expect this, not yet. Sure, they had talked about it, and had decided it would be a good thing to do, but this was happening so fast. He knew he was happy about this, he really was, but there was a nagging sense of worry in the back of his mind. Would he be a good father? Would his darker desires surface around his own child? And what would happen if the police ever discovered what he was doing? What would they do to him or her?

"Wow, I can't believe it. I'm going to be an uncle," Ryan said, a grin plastered on his face.

Samantha beamed, her eyes glistening with joyful tears. "Yes, you are," she said, now wrapping her arms around her brother. "And we're so excited to share this journey with you."

"You're not the only one with a surprise announcement", Ryan said, a smile also on his face.

"I'm sorry", Samantha asked.

"Amanda is pregnant as well."

"Oh Ryan, I'm so happy for you", Samantha said. "Plus I get to be an aunt. I take it you've popped the question?"

"Oh yes, I have. Though...."

"Though what", Samantha asked, raising an eyebrow.

"She wants to move back to New York to be closer to her family. I am seriously considering it."

Samantha seemed to tremble briefly at this, and genuinely seemed conflicted. Suddenly a short, sweet smile came to her face. "Ryan, you need to do whats best for you and your fiancé."

"You sure", Ryan asked.

"Very much so. Vincent and I, we can fly on our own. You need to do what's good for you."

"Thank you Samantha", Ryan said, with a sense of sadness still on his voice. "But enough moping around, this calls for a toast," Ryan declared, raising his glass. Samantha and Vincent raised their glasses as well, clinking them together. The three of them continued to talk and enjoy each other's company before heading their own ways.

Vincent and Samantha sat together in their truck as they drove back to their home.

"So, how are you feeling, hun", Samantha asked, reaching over and giving his hand a squeeze.

"I'm good. Just a little bit shocked is all. But I'm happy, very happy," Vincent replied, giving his wife a reassuring smile.

"That's good," Samantha said, returning a smile.

"How about you? How are you feeling about all of this?", Vincent asked, his tone filled with concern.

"I'm great," Samantha replied. "I'm so excited. And a bit scared, but mostly excited."

"I'm sure you'll be a wonderful mother," Vincent said, his voice filled with sincerity.

"Thanks, hun," Samantha replied, her smile widening.

"So how will this effect our... uhhhh.. special activity?", Vincent asked.

"Oh, well, I'll still be able to help out, don't worry," Samantha said, patting her stomach.

"Are you sure? I don't want you to overexert yourself," Vincent said, his voice filled with concern.

"Well we might have to take it at a reduced rate for a few years, but it's good to take a break sometimes", Samantha said, giving a sly smile to her husband.

"True", Vincent said, agreeing with his wife. It wasn't like he didn't have enough trophies anyway.

He continued to drive home, excited for his future. When they arrived home however, not all was good. The front door was open.

As soon as she saw the lights of the truck, Ann Collins knew she was fucked. Why did she listen to her friend and her boyfriend and break into a taxidermy shop? Now they were in deep shit, and she didn't know what to do. She looked at the door, contemplating whether or not to run.

"Shit, shit, shit," she cursed under her breath.

"What's wrong?", her friend Jessica asked.

"I think someone's coming," Ann replied, her voice laced with panic. Jessica looked at the door and felt her blood turn to ice. She too saw the light of the truck.

"Oh fuck. Oh fuck. What do we do?", Jessica asked, her voice trembling.

"I don't know," Ann replied, her heart racing.

"I think we should run," Jessica suggested.

Ann nodded, grabbing her hand. "Let's go," she said, running towards where the back door should be.

Just as they reached the main hallway, the main entrance opened, and Vincent and Samantha walked in. They quickly turned the other way, looking for another exit, and soon found themselves in a room full of stuffed and taxidermied animals.

"Well, guess we found where they keep the trophies", Jessica joked darkly.

"Really not the time right now Jessica", Ann said panicked.

They were trapped, the only way out being through the door they had just entered through.

"Fuck, we're fucked," Jessica cursed, her voice filled with fear.

"We have to hide," Ann whispered, her eyes darting around the room.

The two young women frantically scanned the room for a hiding spot, their adrenaline pumping. They soon spotted a large cabinet against the wall, and quickly made their way towards it. Ann quickly pulled at it to hide behind, but was surprised that instead of a wooden back wall, she found a hidden passageway.

"What the fuck?", Jessica whispered.

"Get in," Ann commanded, shoving her friend into the passageway. Just as Ann was about to follow, the door to the room opened. She quickly slipped into the passage, shutting the door behind her. The two women stood frozen in the darkness, their hearts pounding, and their breaths ragged.

"Did they see us?", Jessica whispered.

"I don't know, maybe", Ann said, her voice laced with worry.

"Well, I don't want to find out or not, might as well see where this place goes", Jessica said, making her way down the staircase.

"Jessica, wait," Ann hissed, but her friend was already gone.

Ann sighed and followed after her. They soon entered a large, darkened room, with several figure obvious, but unseen due to the lack of light.

"Where are we?", Jessica asked, her voice barely a whisper.

"I don't know, why don't you find a light", Ann asked sarcastically.

"Right, good idea," Jessica replied, feeling along the walls. She soon found one, lighting up the room and its contents.

"What the fuck", Ann said as she stared at a stuffed Girl Scout, forever selling cookies.

"What the hell is this place?", Jessica asked, her voice trembling.

Ann didn't respond, her eyes glued to the lifeless form of the girl. She felt sick to her stomach, her blood running cold. She then looked around and saw several more Girl Scouts in various poses throughout the room. She then saw what looked like a family standing together in a corner, then she saw something that shook her to her core. It was Halie.

"Halie? Is that you? Please be okay, please."

Halie remained silent, her expression blank and unreadable. Ann slowly approached her, her heart pounding.

"Halie, please. It's me, Ann," she said, reaching out a trembling hand. Halie didn't move, her body unnaturally still.

"Oh, God," Ann muttered, her voice cracking. Jessica looked on in shock, her mouth agape.

"Is... is she alive?", Jessica asked, her voice barely a whisper. "I don't know," Ann replied, her voice laced with anguish.

The two young women stood frozen in horror, their hearts racing. Suddenly, the sound of footsteps approaching from behind broke the silence, startling the women. They turned and saw a masked figure standing before them. He was holding what looked like a tranquilizer gun.

"Hello girls" he said before taking aim. Before

the two teens could scream, the man had fired two tranq darts, and things soon went black. Ann could only think about how she got into this situation.

A FEW HOURS EARLIER

Ann Collins was walking down the street with her best friend, Jessica and her boyfriend Jake. It was a beautiful day, the sun was shining, and the air was filled with the scent of freshly cut grass. The brunette wasn't dating anyone, but she was friends with both Jessica and Jake, and didn't mind being a third wheel.

"I can't believe the school year is almost over," Jessica said, a smile on her face.

"Yeah, it's crazy how time flies," Jake agreed.

"I'm so ready for summer break," Ann added, a grin on her face. "I'm hoping I can de-stress, but the way my mom has been acting."

"You like, let her stress get to you", Jake said. He had always been the relaxed laid-back type, and his apparel reflected this. He wore baggy clothes and flip flops everywhere, and his blonde hair was incredibly long.

"So, what do you guys wanna do this weekend?", Jessica asked, looking at her friends, wanting to change the subject to something less depressing.

"I don't know, maybe something that can make us money", Jake said lazily.

"In a single afternoon", Ann questioned.

"Yeah, I'm not sure we can make a lot of money in a single afternoon," Jessica replied, a thoughtful expression on her face.

"Maybe we could, like, start a business or something," Jake suggested, shrugging.

"What kind of business?", Ann asked, her curiosity piqued. "Something that's fun and easy, and makes money," Jake said, as if it were obvious.

"That's a lot of criteria," Jessica commented, an amused smile on her face.

"We could always steal something", Jake suggested.

This gave Ann pause. "Jake, my mom's a cop. I'm going to pretend I didn't hear that."

"Hey, I'm just spit balling here," Jake replied, putting his hands up defensively.

"Well, whatever we do, we have to figure it out fast," Jessica said, checking the time on her phone. "And robbing a house or something just feels wrong, you know."

"Hey, my bother used to do it all the time", Jake exclaimed.

"Isn't your brother doing ten years in the state penitentiary?" Ann asked.

"Yeah, but what if it was someone who deserved it.", Jake said.

"Deserved it? What do you mean by that?", Jessica asked, a curious expression on her face.

"Just, like, someone who's a dick or something," Jake explained, shrugging.

Ann and Jessica exchanged a glance, silently communicating.

"Like, who? Give us some examples," Jessica probed, her voice laced with sarcasm.

"Oh, you know, like that creepy guy who lives a few blocks away. I think he owns a taxidermy shop. We could always take... like... one of his trophies, and I don't think he would miss it.", Jake replied.

"Jake, that's a terrible idea," Ann said, shaking her head.

"It would be funny, though," Jessica countered, her eyes sparkling with mischief.

"Funny? We could get in a lot of trouble. Do you really want to risk it?", Ann asked, incredulous.

"C'mon, it's not like he'll notice. He has, like, a million stuffed animals in there. One missing trophy would go unnoticed," Jessica argued, trying to convince her friend.

"Yeah, I bet. It would be super easy. And the worst that could happen is that we get caught,"

Jake said, his voice nonchalant.

"Exactly," Jessica agreed, nodding her head.

Ann let out a frustrated sigh. "Guys, this is a bad idea," she said, her voice firm.

"Oh, c'mon. Don't be a buzzkill," Jessica replied, rolling her eyes.

"Yeah, Ann. Live a little," Jake said, his tone teasing.

Ann bit her lip, unsure of what to do. A part of her knew this was a bad idea, but the thought of doing something risky and exciting was enticing.

"Fine," she relented, a grin forming on her face. "Let's do it."

"Great. If it makes you feel better, we can just go inside and take a look for now, then come back and do the actual deed later", Jake said.

"Perfect. I can't wait," Jessica said, a mischievous smile on her face.

And that is how the trio ended up at Greenwood Taixdiermy. The two girls would go inside, while Jake would stand watch outside. They had to pry the door open, and Ann was surprised there was no alarm system or anything.

"Wow, this place is creepy," Jessica whispered, her voice filled with awe.

"Yeah, it's like something out of a horror movie," Ann replied, her heart pounding.

The two teens carefully explored the dark

and musty interior of the shop, their footsteps echoing on the dusty floor.

"I'm starting to think this was a bad idea," Ann admitted, a shiver running down her spine.

"Oh, c'mon. Don't be a baby," Jessica replied, her tone teasing. She brushed her blonde hair behind her ear as she said this.

Ann bit her lip, the words stinging. She knew Jessica didn't mean it, but her friend's careless attitude towards the situation made her nervous.

As the two girls continued to explore the shop, the atmosphere began to take a sinister turn. The shadows seemed to grow longer, the air thick with a foreboding sense of dread. The stuffed animals watched them with their hollow eyes, their expressions frozen in a permanent state of mirth.

"We should get out of here," Ann said, her voice trembling. "I've got a bad feeling about this." Suddenly, a light shown in through the window.

"Fuck, someone's coming," Ann hissed, panic seeping into her voice. Ann and Jessica quickly scrambled to find a place to hide, their hearts racing.

LATER THAT NIGHT

Vincent Greenwood stared at the tied up naked body of Ann Collins that lay before him. She was still unconscious and had no idea what awaited her.

"My, my. You are a pretty one, aren't you?", Vincent said, his voice laced with excitement. He grabbed the teens face in his hands and turned her head side to side. Her skin was flawless, her lips plump and inviting. Vincent took a moment to admire the girl's physique, her curves accentuated by the rope binding her. She was young, probably still in high school, and she had a body that any man would be jealous of.

"You're going to look so good stuffed," he murmured, running a hand along her soft skin. "Your two friends will as well", Vincent said. The skinned remains of Jessica Kline and Jake Waters hung from meat hooks a few feet away. Their skin was currently curing in a custom tanning solution to preserve them for evermore.

"Such a shame. You're such a pretty little thing," Vincent said, a wicked smile playing on his lips. He then reached over and grabbed a small knife from his tool table.

"Well, no use wasting time." With that, Vincent took his scalpel and started to make incisions upon the prone girl. He had no way to know, but Ann Collins was actually had regained consciousness, but could not show it. She could only scream internally as she felt every cut made to her body.

CHAPTER 11

Depression

SARAH COLLINS DOWNED another drink of whiskey. It had been one week since her daughter Ann had disappeared, and she was a mess. She knew the statistics of finding her alive were slim at this point. There were no leads, no evidence, nothing.

"Dammit," she muttered, slamming her glass down.

"Whoa, there. Easy," a familiar voice said.

"Ryan, fuck off," Sarah growled, not even turning around to see her partner.

"No can do, partner," Ryan replied, a hint of amusement in his voice. "You look like shit. And smell like shit too."

"Fuck off, Ryan," Sarah repeated, her tone sharp and unfriendly.

"Look, I'm not here to give you a hard time," Ryan said, his voice filled with sincerity. "I'm just worried about you."

"Don't be. I'm fine," Sarah said, her voice strained.

"No, you're not. And I can tell you're drinking too much."

"Am not", Sarah said, slurping her words.

"Sarah, you're a detective. You're not supposed to be lying to people."

"Fuck you," Sarah snapped, glaring at him.

"I'm not the enemy, Sarah."

"Then why aren't you helping me find those Girl Scouts? That family? The rich couple? Or my daughter and her friends?" At this point Sarah broke down crying, and fell from the stool in the bar.

"Sarah, please. Just listen to me," Ryan pleaded, helping his partner up.

"What's there to say? My daughter is dead, Ryan. My baby girl is dead. And I can't do anything to help her," Sarah sobbed, her voice cracking.

"Sarah, that's not true. You're still a detective, you can still help her."

"How? How the fuck am I supposed to do that?", Sarah demanded, her eyes red and puffy. "I have no leads I... I can't even find other people's kids. What hope do I have to find mine? I'm the worst detective in the world."

"Sarah, you can't give up. Not now," Ryan said, his voice filled with conviction.

"And why not? Why the hell not, Ryan?", Sarah demanded, her voice trembling. "I remember you not giving a fuck about these missing people. Why would my daughter change that?"

"Because I know you're better than this, Sarah. I know you can find the answers," Ryan replied, his gaze unwavering.

Sarah scoffed, rolling her eyes. "Don't bullshit me, Ryan," she spat, her tone bitter. "You don't give a shit about my daughter. All you care about is your own career."

"That's not true, Sarah. I care about you, and your family. I'm just trying to help," Ryan protested, his voice laced with hurt.

"Help? Yeah, right. You just want me to get back to work so you don't have to carry my fucking weight."

"Sarah, please. You know that's not true."

"Then why aren't you doing more? Why aren't you out there, looking for her?", Sarah demanded, her voice cracking.

"Because the chief has restricted my access to the case," Ryan replied, his voice quiet.

Sarah scoffed. "The fucking chief. He corrupt as fuck. He has to be. Why deny the obvious?"

"I don't know", Ryan said. He then thought back to something. "You know my parents used it tell me and my sister something growing up."

"What?", Sarah asked, her tone suspicious.

"That everything happens for a reason." Sarah shook her head, a sardonic smile forming on her lips.

"Don't give me that shit, Ryan. You're better than that," she said, her voice laced with contempt.

"Sarah, you have to believe that there's a reason for all of this. You can't just give up," Ryan said, his voice pleading.

"I don't need your goddamn platitudes, Ryan. Just leave me the hell alone," Sarah spat, her voice cold and angry.

Ryan sighed, shaking his head. "I'll see you at work, Sarah. Try and get some rest," he said, his tone defeated.

"Yeah, fuck you," Sarah replied, her words laced with venom.

With that, Ryan turned and walked out of the bar, leaving Sarah alone with her thoughts.

She sat there for a moment, lost in her own world. The weight of the loss hit her once again, and she felt tears welling up in her eyes. She let out a sigh, burying her face in her hands. Ann, where are you?

Vincent Greenwood stepped back from his

latest creation and smiled to himself. Ann Collins simply stared back, a jubilant smile on her face. The brunette was dressed in a pair of denim shorts, a tank top, and a loose flannel shirt, with a pair of cowboy boots on her feet. She was posed as is doing a hoedown, her arms raised and her legs spread apart.

"What do you think, Samantha? Isn't she beautiful?", Vincent asked, his voice filled with pride.

Samantha looked up from her book and smiled. "Yes, hun. She's amazing. You really outdid yourself this time," she said, her tone sincere. "I also like what you did with her friend", Samantha said referring to Jessica.

The blonde girl was posed to be on the wall, like a big mouth bass. The blonde's mouth was open wide, and was dressed in a red swimsuit, her hair in a tight bun. Her boyfriend Jake was posed to be on a surfboard, dressed in nothing but a pair of swim trunks. The three teens did not care about their new positions, as they were no longer capable of doing so.

"Thank you, love," Vincent said, his smile widening.

"I almost forgot", Samantha said, grabbing a newspaper she had been carrying. "These three made the paper, and guess who this one is the daughter of ", she said, jamming her thumb in the direction of Ann.

"Sarah Collins? No way," Vincent replied as he scanned over the paper, his tone filled with surprise.

"Yep, her daughter is Ann Collins," Samantha said, nodding her head.

"Well, I'll be damned," Vincent muttered, shaking his head. "She has no idea her daughter is right under her nose."

"Yeah, I wonder how she's taking this," Samantha said, her voice laced with curiosity.

"Well, if she's anything like her daughter, she's not taking it well," Vincent replied, a sly smile etched on his lips. "Perhaps we should be on the lookout for detective Collins, it could be a good way to reunite the two."

"Yeah, maybe," Samantha agreed, her tone thoughtful.

Vincent smiled to himself, a plan already formulating in his mind. "Well, I better get back to work," he said, picking up his tools. "I've got a charity auction I need to prepare for."

"Okay, hun. Good luck," Samantha replied, giving him a quick kiss. "I still want to do those med students."

"Oh, we will, don't worry about that. We just need to wait for things to cool down a bit."

Vincent then headed out of the room, a wicked smile on his face. "Soon, Sarah Collins. "Soon."

Sarah Collins sat at her desk, staring blankly at her computer screen. It had been two weeks since her daughter had gone missing, and the only thing she had managed to accomplish was an alcohol habit.

"Jesus Christ, Sarah. Pull yourself together," she muttered, running a hand through her hair.

"Hey, you doing okay?", Ryan asked, taking a seat at his desk.

"I'm fine," Sarah grumbled, not bothering to look up from her computer.

"Bullshit. You're a fucking mess, Sarah," Ryan said, his tone blunt.

"What's your fucking problem, Ryan? Can't you leave me alone for five minutes?"

Ryan put his fingers on his temples in frustration, and took a deep breath. "I want to let you know this is my last week here."

"Wait, what?", Sarah asked, her eyes widening.

"Yeah, I'm moving to New York and I am joining the NYPD."

"Why the fuck are you doing that?", Sarah asked, incredulous.

"Because my fiancée is pregnant, and she

wants to move back to the city to be with her family."

Sarah bit her lip, feeling guilty.

"Shit, Ryan. I'm sorry. I didn't know," she said, her voice laced with remorse.

"It's okay. I wasn't planning on telling anyone but my sister until after my last day, but you're my partner, and you deserve to know."

"So, this is really it, huh?", Sarah asked, a sad smile on her face.

"Yeah, it is," Ryan replied, a similar expression on his face.

"Well, I guess I'll miss you, you asshole," Sarah said, chuckling.

"I'll miss you too, Sarah. You're a great detective," Ryan replied, his tone sincere. "I know you will find Ann and those girls, just not with me."

"Thanks, Ryan. And I wish you the best of luck with your family," Sarah said, her smile widening.

"Thank you, Sarah," Ryan replied, a smile tugging at his lips.

Sarah reached out and grabbed his hand, giving it a firm squeeze. "Take care, Ryan. And be safe," she said, her voice serious.

"You too, Sarah," Ryan said, returning her gesture.

With that, Ryan got up from his chair and began to gather his belongings. He stopped and looked at Sarah once more. "Sarah, you can do this. I believe in you," he said, his voice filled with confidence.

"Thanks, Ryan. Now get the fuck out of here," Sarah said, laughing.

"Yes, ma'am," Ryan said, saluting her.

With that, he turned and walked out of the precinct.

Sarah watched him go, a wistful expression on her face. She knew she would miss him, but she also knew he was right. She could do this. She had to. For Ann's sake.

Samantha Greenwood smiled as she drove home. This was her first solo hunting trip, and she would say it was a success. She glanced in her rearview mirror at the two lumps under a blanket in the backseat. She had decided to take two med students on her hunt, having found they complimented each other, plus they were sisters to boot. They had no idea what awaited them, and Samantha loved the idea of their reactions.

"Oh, you are going to love your new home," she said, her tone filled with excitement.

The two sisters were silent, their heads

lolling side to side as the car drove on.

"This is going to be so much fun," Samantha said, her eyes sparkling with mischief.

She soon pulled up to her and her husband's home and quickly parked the car. She then got out and opened the back door, removing the blanket from her prizes. The two young women were still dressed in their blue hospital scrubs, their brown hair pulled back in ponytail's. Their bodies were limp, their expressions blank.

"Come on, you two. Let's get you inside," Samantha said, grabbing their arms and pulling them out of the car.

She carried their limp bodies inside one at a time, and down to her husbands workshop, where they were tied up. Soon, they would become masterpieces, and be added to their growing collection. Soon.

CHAPTER 12

Suspicion

DETECTIVE SARAH COLLINS was a mess. Her hair was unkempt, her eyes were red and puffy from crying, and she hadn't showered in days. It had been three weeks since her daughter had gone missing, and she hadn't found any new leads. Her partner was gone, and she was sure the chief wanted to fire her after her outburst in his office.

"Collins, you're going to have to lay off these 'missing persons' cases for a while."

"Why, chief ?", Sarah asked, her voice laced with suspicion.

"I have my reasons. Just do it, Collins. You're on thin ice here," the chief said, his voice firm.

"Sir, if I may, my daughter is one of these missing persons."

The chief scoffed at this. "Oh, come on Collins, do you really think someone kidnapped her. She's a teenager, probably just away. Same with those girl scouts."

Sarah clenched her fists, her nails digging into her palms.

"How can you say that sir? They're kids, they wouldn't just run away," Sarah protested, her voice laced with anger. "Plus, I know my Ann, she wouldn't run away either."

"Listen, Collins. I've heard enough," the chief said, his tone final. "There is nothing going on here, this is a safe town."

"But, sir-" Sarah tried to protest, but the chief cut her off.

"That's enough. You're on suspension until further notice. Go home and get some rest, you're a fucking mess."

"Fine," Sarah grumbled, turning and storming out of the chief's office. She knew the chief was hiding something, she could feel it in her bones. There was no way the missing people weren't connected, and she was going to prove it. She had to.

Returning to the present, Sarah was left with only her thoughts. Besides trying to find the missing people, she had done some research into the chiefs background, and found nothing. Best she could tell, he always kept his head down, and did it enough to come eventually come into a position of power. The thought of that man dismissing her like that, this just made her blood boil.

Sarah looked at a framed photo of Ann longingly. Well, if she wasn't a cop anymore, and she hasn't been called back yet, then there's nothing stopping her from going scorched earth on this case. Rules, regulations, they were all out the window. She would find Ann and bring her home. No matter the cost.

Samantha Greenwood hummed a tune as she dusted off her husband's collection of taxidermied humans. It had been a month since she had her solo hunting trip, and it was nice to see the finished products. She looked over at the two med students, now a pair of stuffed sisters. They were posed to be having a conversation, their hands gesturing as they spoke. Not a hint of concern was on their squarish faces.

"You two are so cute," Samantha cooed, a smile on her face. She brushed her hand on the older sister's check, her name had been Becca, her brown hair hung loose upon her shoulders.

"I wish I could talk to you two," she said, her tone wistful. Samantha sighed, turning her attention to the younger sister, named Rae, her light brown hair was tied in a braid. She wondered what they would say to her, if they could speak. Would they call her crazy? Maybe even beg her for mercy. The thought made her heart race, a sense of anticipation rising within her.

"It's a shame you can't talk. I bet you would have a lot to say," Samantha mused, her voice laced with disappointment. She turned and looked around the room, at all the lifeless eyes staring back at her. "I wonder if you would all say the same thing. That I'm crazy."

The stuffed figures remained silent, for many, their expressions frozen in a state of permanent joy.

"Well, whatever. I'm not crazy," Samantha said, shrugging. She walked over to the two girls, giving them both a pat on the head. "You guys are just jealous."

With that, Samantha turned and walked out of the room, leaving the two med students alone with their fellow trophies.

Sarah Collins stared at the map of the surrounding area. Her desk was covered in notes, files, and empty coffee cups. It had been a week since her suspension, and she was determined to find answers.

"Come on, there has to be something," Sarah muttered, her voice filled with frustration. She scanned the map, looking for anything that might stand out.

"Dammit." Nothing made sense. Her daughter was gone, those girls were gone, and she could do nothing to find them. As it turns out, detective work without a partner or actual institutional backing was hard. She really wished she was Sherlock Holmes at the moment, then she would solve the case at the end of the book, instead she felt like she was in a Greek tragedy.

"Fuck this," Sarah growled, her temper flaring. She picked up a file and threw it across the room, the papers flying everywhere. "Fuck!"

Sarah fell to her knees, tears streaming down her face. She had failed. She had failed as a mother, and as a detective. She was a failure.

"I'm so sorry, Ann," Sarah sobbed, her body trembling. "I'm so sorry." She hated the chief, she hated this town, she wanted answers, but no one wanted the truth.

Sarah's teary eyes wandered the mess on the floor, when she spotted something. She reached her shaking hand over to it and pulled it closer to her. It was a transcript of her interview with Samantha Anderson... no Greenwood. She was the last to see those girls scouts alive, she knew something but wasn't telling. Suddenly it hit her like a ton of bricks, that woman's house wasn't far from where Ann had last been seen. Maybe, just maybe, the two were connected.

Sarah wiped the tears from her face and got up. She had a lead.

Samantha Greenwood sat at her computer, a smile on her face. She and Vincent agreed to lay low for a while after the two medical students. She was amazed that the police still hadn't connected all of these disappearances together. She had no idea what was on the new mayor or the chief of police's minds. Even though they refused to do anything about it, they couldn't just become complacent like that could they? No, they needed to be careful and sneaky.

Samantha felt a kick and looked down at her baby bump. She was only 18 weeks along, and already starting to show. She and Vincent were both excited for the baby to arrive, and couldn't wait to add an-other member to their family.

Samantha's thoughts were interrupted by a knock at the door. "Who the hell could that be?", she muttered, getting up and making her way to the front door.

As Samantha opened the door, she was greeted by a familiar face. "Hello, Mrs. Greenwood. Do you have a minute?", Sarah asked, a fake smile on her face.

"Sure, come on in," Samantha replied, a curious expression on her face.

The two women walked into the living room, their steps echoing on the hardwood floor.

"So, what brings you here, Detective Collins?", Samantha asked, her tone friendly.

"Well, I just wanted to ask you a few questions about the night those Girl Scouts went missing," Sarah explained, her tone professional.

"Again?" Samantha asked, confused. It was then that she noticed the detective wasn't wearing a uniform or even in professional clothing. Instead she was dressed in a pair of blue jeans and a simple blue t-shirt.

"Yes, again. I know it's been a few months, but I just want to make sure we didn't miss anything," Sarah replied, her voice sincere.

"Well, okay," Samantha said, shrugging. "I don't know how much help I can be, but I'll do my best."

"Great, thank you," Sarah said, her smile widening. The two women sat down, their eyes locked on each other.

"Now", Detective Collins asked, staying professional, "can you tell me what happened that night?"

"Well, I took the girls to the camp site, as as we set up, I realized we were missing a few items, and left the oldest girl in charge while I drove back to town to get said items. By time I got back, all the girls were just gone."

"I see," Sarah said, her eyes narrowing.

"Is there something wrong, Detective Collins?", Samantha asked, her tone innocent.

"No, not at all," Sarah replied, shaking her head. "It's just..."

"It's just what?", Samantha asked, somewhat concerned.

"Nothing, it's nothing," Sarah said, waving her hand dismissively.

"Are you sure, Detective Collins? You seem troubled."

"I'm fine, I promise," Sarah assured, her smile forced.

"Well, okay," Samantha said, clearly not believing her.

"Now, can you tell me what you did after the Girl Scouts went missing?", Sarah asked, her tone serious.

"I called the police, and then I waited. When they arrived, I explained what happened, and they took down my statement. That was the end of it."

"Hmm, alright. Did you notice anything

strange that night?"

"No, nothing at all."

"Well, all right then", Detective Collins said with a sickly sweet smile that was clearly fake. "I think that covers all of our bases."

"I should hope so", Samantha said, clearly annoyed.

With that, Samantha walked the detective out and closed the door, making sure to lock it. She waited for the detective to leave before taking in a deep breath. She needed to tell Vincent what had happened, and fast.

It had taken all of Sarah's will to not punch that woman in the face. She was guilty as hell, and she knew it. Though no actual hard evidence existed, she just had a gut feeling.

Sarah climbed into her car and pulled out her phone, dialing the chief's number.

"Hello?", a gruff voice answered.

"Chief, it's me," Sarah said, her tone firm.

"Why are you calling me in the middle of dinner, your suspended remember."

"Yes, I remember. But I think I have a lead on the case."

"What?", the chief asked, incredulous.

"You're still working the case, even after I suspended you?"

"Yeah, well, fuck the rules. My daughter is missing, and you refuse to acknowledge that."

The chief sighed, his tone exasperated, and filled with contempt. "Well too fucking bad. And you know what, your fired."

"Oh, you're not firing me," Sarah replied, her voice confident.

"The hell I'm not," the chief growled, his anger rising.

"Not until you admit what's going on here. Something's wrong in this town, and you know it."

"You're a lunatic," the chief spat, his voice filled with contempt.

"Am I? Then explain why you keep covering this up," Sarah demanded, her voice growing louder.

"There's nothing to cover up Collins. The case is closed, and you're fired. I'm hanging up now, and don't call me again, or I'll have you arrested," the chief said, his tone final.

"Wait, dammit!" The line went dead. Sarah was now daughterless and jobless. She had nothing.

She gripped the steering wheel, her knuckles white. She was not going to let this go. She would find her daughter, and she would expose the truth. No matter what.

With that, Sarah started her car and drove off into the night, the darkness closing in around her. She had nothing to lose anymore. She was going to find Ann, even if it was the last thing she ever did.

CHAPTER 13

Confrontations

LATER THAT NIGHT

Former detective Sarah Collins pulled up to the Greenwood house, her headlights off, moving at a slow speed. She didn't want anyone to know she was here. She didn't want to take any chances.

Sarah parked her car a few houses down and made her way on foot. The night was dark, the stars hidden by the clouds, with no moon in the sky. She kept to the shadows, her heart pounding.

"Here goes nothing," she muttered, as she stepped onto the porch of the Greenwood house.

She quickly checked the door, which was

locked. "Damn it." She should of known better, and that it would be locked.

Sarah glanced around, making sure no one was watching. She then moved to a nearby window and tried to open it. No luck.

"Shit," she swore, her voice a harsh whisper. She looked around once more, her eyes darting around the darkness. She then reached into her pocket and pulled out a lockpick, a skill she had learned a few years ago.

With a few deft motions, Sarah managed to pick the lock and opened the door. It slowly creaked open, Sarah not wanting to make any noise. She creeped her way into the house, slowly looking around the corner for any activity. There was none, which was not surprising considered the late hour it was.

Sarah snuck her way into the living room, her eyes scanning the dark interior. She moved over to a nearby desk and began rifling through the various knickknacks.

"Come on, there has to be something," she muttered, her voice barely above a whisper. Opening one of the drawers of the desk, she is surprised to find it is full of wallets and deactivated cell phones.

"What the hell?", she murmured, her brows furrowing. She then picked up one of the wallets and opened it.

Her eyes widened as she saw a familiar face

staring back at her. It was Ann. She would recognize her anywhere.

"Oh my god," she gasped, her hand flying to her mouth. "Oh, Ann." She then picked up another wallet and saw another familiar face. Jessica Kline.

"This is not happening," Sarah muttered, her mind racing.

She continued searching the drawers and found even more wallets and cell phones. She was horrified at what she was finding.

"What the fuck is going on here?", she wondered, her voice a harsh whisper. She had suspected Samantha and her husband had something to do with this, but evidence still shook her to her core. Of course none of this was admissible in court, but she would deal her own justice to these bastards.

Moving away from the desk, Sarah headed for an ajar door, and found herself in a trophy room full of taxidermied animals. This must save the showroom for the taxidermy shop. But there must be more,
there had to be.

As Sarah made her way though the room, she tried to find any hidden doors or controls, and was surprised to find that the bookshelf was on a rail.

"Jackpot," she whispered, her tone triumphant.

She pulled the bookshelf open, revealing a hidden staircase that seemed to have no visible end. The first thing Sarah noticed was the smell. A coppery scent filled her nostrils, and she felt bile rising in her throat.

"Oh my god," she moaned, her voice choked with horror. As she stepped into the abyss, her eyes were wide with fear.

"What the hell is this place?", she muttered, her voice barely a whisper. Slowly she made her way down into the darkness, with only a flashlight for company. Eventually this leveled out into what appeared to be a second hidden trophy room. Shining her flashlight around, Sarah's blood ran cold when it fell upon a small figure dressed in a classic green Girl Scout uniform.

"Oh god, no," she whimpered, her voice cracking. She walked up to the lifeless girl, her heart pounding.

"It can't be," she muttered, her voice filled with denial. As she got closer, she saw a name tag sewn into the girl's uniform. It read 'Emma'.

"Oh, no," Sarah groaned, her hands flying to her mouth.

She looked over the stuffed girl scout, and saw her eyes were open, but empty.

"Oh, Emma," Sarah whispered, her voice filled with grief.

She then noticed the other figures in the

room, and felt the bile rise in her throat once more. There were the rest of the missing Girl Scouts, posed doing different things, all lifeless.

"Fuck, fuck, fuck," Sarah swore, her voice a harsh whisper. She could no longer hold back the tears, and they fell freely down her cheeks.

Sarah turned and hurried back the way she came, her mind racing. It was at that moment that she ran into the missing Gardner family, causing small Anna Gardner to wobble in place. Sarah did her best to steady the girl to keep her from falling down.

"I'm so sorry, little one," she apologized, her voice shaky. Anna just looked at her with blank eyes, not a care in the world. Sarah for her part was shaking, evident by the tremble in her hands.

"Jesus, oh Jesus," she moaned, her voice laced with panic. She took a few steps back, and bumped into another statue, a teenage boy dressed only in a bathing suit. Suddenly Sarah recognized the boy, him being a friend of Ann. "Jake," she said, this being the only thing she could say.

Moving the flashlight around, she sees mounted on the wall like a fish was Jessica, the blonde's mouth open like a bass.

"I can't...," Sarah stammered, her mind racing. "This is not..." She took a few deep breaths, trying to calm herself. "Oh, my god," she whispered, her voice a harsh whisper. She desperately didn't want to imagine who she would find next, but all but knew it was inevitable. Turning her flashlight, she is met by a figure posed to be dancing that made her drop her flashlight. It was Ann.

"No," Sarah gasped, trying her hardest not to break down, her voice barely a whisper. "No!"

Sarah felt the tears stream down her cheeks, her body trembling. "Ann," she sobbed, her voice choked with grief. Ann was posed like a cowgirl, with one leg raised. Sarah knew her daughter hated country music, and would have hated how she was posed, putting aside the horrifying fact of what happened to her.

Sarah fell to her knees, her mind numb. She had failed. She had lost her daughter, and she had failed to protect her.

"Oh, Ann," she whimpered, her body wracked with guilt Sarah buried her face in her hands, her shoulders shaking. She had nothing left.

Suddenly, the lights flickered on, and Sarah was bathed in light.

"I'm so sorry, detective," a familiar voice said, her tone filled with regret. Sarah turned trying to find the person speaking, but was unsuccessful. Suddenly she felt a prick in her neck. Suddenly, everything went dark.

Sarah Collins was groggy as she awoke. Perhaps all of this was a bad dream? She tried to roll over but found that she couldn't.

"What", she said in a tired hoarse voice, and tried to open her eyes, but her vision was still blurry. Soon this adjusted and Sarah could see better. The room she was in was bare, with only a single light hanging from the ceiling.

Looking around, Sarah was horrified to see the same lifeless eyes of the girl scouts staring back at her.

"After all the effort you went to finding them, I thought you would like to see them properly", a mysterious voice said calmly.

Turning her head, she could see Samantha Greenwood and her husband Vincent.

"You," Sarah hissed, her eyes narrowing.

Samantha sighed, a disappointed look on her face. "I was really hoping we wouldn't have to do this," she said, her tone resigned.

"You killed them," Sarah growled, her eyes blazing with rage.

"No, I didn't. Well... O.K maybe I did, but I gave them freedom from the horrors of aging.", Vincent said, trying to defend himself.

"You turned them into your own personal

trophies. You are a sick son of a bitch," Sarah spat, her voice laced with anger.

"That's not true," Samantha protested, her eyes flashing. "They will retain their innocence and youth and will be together forever. It is so much better this way."

"You're crazy," Sarah whispered, her voice now filled with horror.

"I prefer the term, creative," Vincent replied, an evil smile on his face.

"This ends now," Sarah growled, her voice fierce.

"Said the woman who is tied naked to a chair", Vincent said sarcastically.

Sarah looked down and was horrified to find that she was in fact naked and tied to a chair, just as the madman had said. She couldn't even cover herself and was forced to give these perverts a free peep show.

"So, what now?", she demanded, her voice wavering slightly.

"Well, we can't have you running off and telling the world about us," Vincent said, his tone serious. "But think of it this way, your beauty will be preserved and you get to be reunited with your daughter... forever"

"You're sick," Sarah hissed, her eyes narrowed.

"No, I'm just doing what needs to be done,"

Vincent replied, his expression solemn.

"I'm sorry, Sarah. But it's the only way," Samantha said, her voice filled with sadness.

"You will never get away with this," Sarah snarled, her tone defiant.

"Actually, we already have," Vincent said, a smirk on his face. "You see I've been doing this for years now, though troupe 1472 is probably my greatest masterpiece. They did get the most attention after all.

"I'm sure you were real proud of yourself, you fucking asshole," Sarah spat.

"Hey, hey, watch the language," Vincent chided, a grin on his face. "There are children here", he said as he indicated the taxidermied Girl Scouts.

"Fuck you," Sarah hissed, her voice venomous.

"You're feisty, I'll give you that," Vincent said with amusement.

"Don't worry, Sarah. This will all be over soon," Samantha assured the former detective, a sad smile on her face.

"You're crazy if you think I'm going to let you turn me into a taxidermied piece of art."

"That's where you're wrong, Detective Collins. You don't have a choice in the matter," Vincent replied, his tone serious.

Sarah struggled against her bonds, but they were too strong. She was trapped.

"Please, let me go," she begged, her voice laced with desperation.

"We can't do that," Vincent said, his tone final.

"But we will give you one last chance to say goodbye to your daughter," Samantha added, as she walked into another room. She soon returned wheeling in the stiffened form of her daughter.

"Ann," Sarah sobbed, her voice breaking. "Oh, Ann." She stared at her daughter's frozen form, her heart palpitating. "I'm so sorry, sweetheart. I failed you," she whispered, tears streaming down her face.

Vincent rolled his eyes. "Enough of this," he said, his voice exasperated. He then began to approach the woman, a needle in his hand.

"Wait, wait", Sarah pleaded, her voice frantic.

"No more waiting," Vincent replied, his tone final.

Before Sarah could protest further, Vincent plunged the needle into her neck, injecting her with a powerful sedative.

"Don't worry, Detective. You won't feel a thing," Vincent said, his voice laced with mock concern.

"You bastard," Sarah slurred, her vision beginning to fade once more.

"Goodbye, Detective. Thank you for your service," Vincent said, a smug smile on his face.

Sarah tried to reply, but the darkness was closing in around her. She looked at her daughter one last time, her heart heavy.

"I'm sorry, Ann," she whispered. She then slumped over.

Vincent Greenwood was taking in the smell of his latest culinary masterpiece, jambe si détective. After skinning Sarah Collins, he still had her flesh, which he didn't want to go to waist. He just hoped she tasted as good as her daughter did.

After over two hours of cooking, Vincent pulled his roast out of the oven. The left leg of Sarah Collins was cooked to perfection and was a nice crispy brown.

"Exquisite," he said, a smile on his face. He then speed walked into the dining room, carrying his roast and setting it on a heat proof lazy susan.

Samantha, meanwhile, who had been setting the table, was now looking over her husband's handiwork.

"Looks delicious," she said, her voice filled with pride.

"Why thank you, my dear," Vincent replied,

his tone appreciative.

"Only the best for the best," Samantha said, smiling.

"Now, let's eat," Vincent said, his stomach rumbling. The two sat down and began to enjoy their meal.

"This is wonderful," Samantha said, her voice filled with delight.

"I agree. Detective Collins does make a delicious meal," Vincent replied, a smirk on his face. "We should thank her after dinner."

Samantha laughed, her eyes sparkling. "Indeed we should," she said, a mischievous smile on her face.

As the two finished their meal, they were sated and content. Little was left of the leg, though the rest of her meat was in the fridge. She did in fact taste just as good as her daughter. Once they had cleaned up the dinning room and the kitchen, the two headed down to the workshop, where the taxidermied form of Sarah Collins stood.

"So, what do you think?", Vincent asked, his tone curious.

"She's beautiful," Samantha replied, her voice filled with admiration. The lifeless eyes of Sarah Collins stared back at them, her expression frozen in determination. She was posed with her feet apart, her weapon raised in front of her. She was dressed in the clothes she had been wearing when captured.

"You did a great job," Samantha complimented, a smile on her face. "So who do you think is next to join our little collection?"

"Oh, who knows. But until then, we have plenty of other guests to keep us company," Vincent said, a smug smile on his face.

"And many more to come", Samantha said, hugging her husband from behind before kissing him on the neck.

Life was good for Vincent, life was very good.

PART II

CHAPTER 14

Family Man

THE CRIES OF JEREMY Greenwood woke his parents for the third time that night. It was Vincent's turns to calm him down. He deliriously rolled out of bed and headed to the nursery. He wished he had known that being a parent would be this hard.

Opening the door, the cries got louder. Jeremy had managed to kick off his blankets, and was crying up a storm.

"Shh, shh, it's alright, buddy," Vincent said, his voice gentle. He was currently holding his son in his arms, trying to calm him down. It was at this point that he smelled something.

"Oh, geez," he muttered, his nose wrinkling. He then carried the baby over to the changing table and quickly changed the diaper. This in itself was not that out of the ordinary, but what was out of the ordinary was the changing table itself, with it being built out of a taxidermied family he had acquired recently. The table was built from the mom and dad (Mary and Frank) , while their 14 year old daughter (Alexa) stood to the side, holding a fresh diaper. He had spotted the family one day at a charity breakfast and had followed them home, they certainly had no complaints about the arrangement.

Jeremy looked around the room, his eyes wide. He seemed to be taking in his surroundings, and Vincent knew the baby had no idea what was going on. He was only three weeks old after all.

"Let's get you back to bed," Vincent said, his voice gentle. He gently rocked the baby, his hands warm. Jeremy cooed softly, his eyes half-closed.

Vincent walked over to the crib and gently placed the baby down. He then grabbed the blanket and covered the baby, making sure to tuck him in.

"There you go, little man," Vincent said, his voice soothing. Jeremy yawned, his eyes closed. Vincent smiled and kissed his son on the forehead, his lips soft.

"Sleep tight, buddy," he whispered, his voice filled with affection. Vincent slowly walked out of the room, quietly closing the door behind him. He soon crawled back into bed and fell asleep himself. This was tiring work, but worth it.

Vincent woke up a few hours later, his head groggy. He looked over at the clock, and saw that it was 5:30 am. He groaned, and rolled over, hoping to get some more sleep. As he did so, he was greeted by a pair of familiar arms wrapping around him.

"Good morning, sunshine," a voice said, her tone playful. "Good morning," Vincent replied, his voice tired.

"I made some coffee, if you want some," Samantha offered, her voice gentle.

"Yeah, I think I could use some," Vincent agreed, his tone appreciative.

"Alright, let's go," Samantha said, her voice cheerful. The husband and wife duo soon headed down to the kitchen wear the coffee was poured, before sitting at a table and enjoying each others company.

"So, what do you think about the nursery?", Vincent asked, his voice curious.

"It's wonderfull" Samantha replied, her voice filled with wonder. "They're beautiful", she added.

"I'm glad you think so," Vincent said, a smile on his face.

"You've really outdone yourself this time," Samantha praised, a smile on her face.

"I try," Vincent replied, a shrug.

"Do you think he'll like it?", Samantha asked, her tone hopeful.

"Who, Jeremy? I'm sure he will," Vincent said, his tone reassuring.

"I can't wait for him to meet everyone," Samantha said, her eyes sparkling.

"When he is older" Vincent said with a smile, fantasizing about that day.

"He's going to have such an amazing family," Samantha said, her voice filled with excitement.

"Yes, he is," Vincent agreed, a smirk on his face. Suddenly, a cry came from upstairs.

"I better go get that", Samantha said, getting up and leaving her coffee behind.

Vincent watched his wife head upstairs, a smile on his face. He was excited for the future, and for Jeremy. He had no idea what would await him.

As Vincent sipped his coffee, he heard the faint sound of laughter coming from the nursery. Life was good.

Two Months Later

Vincent Greenwood walked through his house, his mind racing. He had just gotten a call from his wife, telling him to come home. It had sounded urgent, and he had dropped everything and headed home. He soon arrived, and made his way inside.

"Samantha?", he called out, his voice echoing through the house.

"In the living room," she replied, her voice distant.

Vincent headed towards the living room, his steps hurried. He was soon met with the sight of his wife and their infant son, who were currently sitting in a rocking chair.

"Hey, what's going on?", Vincent asked, his voice concerned.

"Guess what?" She said, barely hiding her smile.

"What?", Vincent asked, his brow furrowing.

"I'm pregnant again," Samantha said.

"Really?" Vincent replied in disbelief, his eyes widening.

"Mmhmm," Samantha replied, a smile on her face.

"Oh my God," Vincent said, his voice filled

with shock.

"Isn't it wonderful?", Samantha asked, her tone excited.

"Yeah, it is," Vincent replied, his mind still processing the news.

"I can't wait to tell everyone," Samantha said, her tone enthusiastic. "I've already told all the trophies."

"I don't think they can hear you", Vincent said chuckling.

"Oh, you know what I mean", Samantha said playfully.

"I'm happy for you," Vincent said, a smile on his face.

"I'm happy for us," Samantha replied, her eyes sparkling.

"This is going to be great," Vincent said, his voice filled with anticipation.

"Yeah, it is," Samantha agreed, her smile widening.

With the prospect of a new addition to his family on the horizon, Vincent could not help but be excited. He had big hopes for his growing family and couldn't wait to see where they would take him.

It was good sometimes to take a break. It had been over a year since Vincent had gone human hunting and made a new trophy, and for a good reason at that. After all, he was now the father of three young children (Jermey the oldest, and the twins Leah and Thomas). He knew he couldn't risk getting caught and leaving his family unsupported.

"Penny for your thoughts", the voice of his wife called out, making him snap back to reality.

"Huh, what?", Vincent said, his mind racing.

"Penny for your thoughts. Whatcha thinking about?", Samantha repeated, a smile on her face.

"Oh, uh, nothing really. Just lost in thought," Vincent replied, giving a shrug.

"O.K", Samantha said, sitting down next to her husband. "Do you miss it sometimes?", she asked.

"Miss what?", Vincent asked, his brow furrowing.

"Human hunting", Samantha clarified, her tone serious.

"Ah, yeah. Sometimes I do. But I have responsibilities now, you and the kids always come first."

"Ahh, you're so sweet". Samantha said, kissing Vincent. "Though... when do you think you'll do it again."

"I don't know. Maybe soon. I haven't decided yet," Vincent replied, his tone thoughtful.

"Well, I can't wait to see the next one," Samantha said, her voice filled with excitement.

"Thanks, babe," Vincent said, a smile on his face.

Samantha leaned against her husband, her head resting on his shoulder.

"I love you," she whispered, her voice gentle.

"I love you, too," Vincent replied, his tone sincere.

The couple sat in silence, enjoying each others company. The moment was perfect, and neither wanted it to end.

***

Two Years Later

Thanks to the work of detective Sarah Collins before her disappearance, everyone knew that the town of Pinehurst had a serial killer among its ranks, well everyone but the chief of police and Mayor, who both remained in denial. But for the past four years going on five years, things had been quiet. Trust in others had been rebuilt, and people were moving on with their lives. The chief had won, and public order was restored. Though things would soon change, once Vincent Greenwood had an idea for a project in mind.

"What do you think?", Vincent asked his wife, his tone eager as he showed her some reconnaissance photos he had taken.

"I love them," Samantha replied, her voice filled with excitement.

"It's going to be amazing," Vincent said, his tone confident.

"How soon can we start?", Samantha asked, her tone excited.

"Soon, very soon," Vincent replied, a smirk on his face.

"Oh, I can't wait," Samantha said, her eyes sparkling.

"We're going to have so much fun," Vincent said, his eyes darkening with excitement.

"I know," Samantha replied, her voice filled with anticipation.

Vincent smiled, his mind racing. He longingly looked at the photos once more. He was going to make his return in a big way. In the photo, the Pinehurst high varsity cheer team was practicing their routine, unaware they were being hunted.

CHAPTER 15

School Spirit

THE PINEHURST HIGH Varsity Cheerleaders certainly weren't the best in the nation, but they got the job done. Besides, they were still in the top ten in the state. It was a sunny afternoon, and the girls were practicing their routine for the big game that weekend.

"Alright, ladies, let's take it from the top," the captain, Paige O'Hara, called out, her voice authoritative.

"Yes, Captain," the girls replied in unison, their voices obedient. The girls took their positions and began their routine. They were focused, their movements precise.

"That's it, ladies, you're doing great," Paige encouraged, her voice filled with pride.

The girls continued their practice, their spirits high. They knew they had a chance to make it to the nationals this year.

"Take five, ladies," Paige called out, her voice tired. She, along with the rest of her teammates were hot and sweaty.

The girls took a break, their breaths heavy. They sat down on the bleachers and took a sip of water, their eyes bright. What none of them realized was that they were being watched. Yes, they expected spectators, but this spectator was different, and they were none the wiser.

The locker room for the cheerleaders was hot and steamy, it was always like this after practice, and was filled to the brim with teenage girls changing into their regular clothes.

"Perfect", said Vincent Greenwood, as he watched from the locked coach's office. The man was wearing a full hazmat suit and a rebreather, as he prepared to collect his bounty.

He had been planning this for a while and was ready. He watched the girls undress, his eyes darkening with lust. Their bodies were toned and athletic, and their skin glistened with sweat.

"Mmm," Vincent murmured, his voice appreciative. He couldn't wait to get his hands on them.

Suddenly a hissing sound could be heard, as a nerve toxin flooded the room. The cheerleaders coughed and gasped, their bodies wracked with spasms.

"What's... what's going on?", Paige choked out, her voice strained.

The girls struggled to stay conscious, but it was a losing battle. One by one they fell to the floor, their eyes rolling back in their heads.

"Gotcha," Vincent muttered, a smirk on his face.

He opened the door to the office and stepped into the locker room. He quickly scanned the scene and saw that the girls were unconscious. Perfect.

He grabbed the nearest girl and dragged her towards the coach's office. According to his research, her name was Maya. She was a redhead, with blue eyes and freckles on her face. He soon dragged her inside and laid her down, her body limp.

"What a pretty little thing you are," he murmured, his voice filled with admiration. Not wanting to waste any time, he picked her up over his shoulder and brought her to the coaches private entrance, where a van was waiting. He placed the unconscious teen in the back before returning for her teammates.

One by one he loaded the girls into the back of the van, until only Paige was left.

"Time to go home," Vincent murmured, his voice laced with excitement.

He grabbed Paige and hauled her towards the coach's office, her body limp. She was a blonde with blue eyes and a slim figure. She had been the captain of the cheer squad and had led them to great victories. "Let's see how well you lead your team now," Vincent muttered, a smirk on his face.

With all the cheerleaders secure in the van, he shut the doors and hopped in the driver's seat.

"Time for the fun to begin," he said, his voice dark. He put the van in drive and headed off into the sunset.

Eighteen-year-old Paige O'Hara stirred and was a bit groggy. She tried to roll over but found that she couldn't.

"Huh? What the?", she said, her voice filled with confusion.

She soon noticed her surroundings. The room was dark and cold, and there was a low hum of electricity. Looking down, she saw that she was naked and strapped to some sort of table.

"What the fuck!" She shouted.

"Shhh", a deep voice said. "There's no need to use that type of language young lady." Stepping out of the shadows was Vincent Greenwood, not that Paige knew who he was.

"What is this?", she demanded, "Who are you?" her voice filled with fear.

"Oh, it's nothing," Vincent said, his voice smooth.

"Nothing? I'm tied up and naked! This is not nothing," Paige protested, her voice rising.

"You're not the first," Vincent said, his tone amused.

"What the hell does that mean?", Paige asked, her voice wavering.

"It means that you're just the latest addition to my collection," Vincent replied, his eyes glittering.

"Your collection? What are you talking about?", Paige demanded.

Vincent sighed. "Let me show you." With that he turned and left the room. When he returned, he was wheeling in a cart with a naked figure on it, who Paige recognized.

"Maya?", Paige asked, her voice a strangled whisper as she recognized her teammate.

"Indeed," Vincent replied, his tone casual. "She's a beauty, isn't she?"

Paige stared at her friend, her eyes wide. Maya for her part only stared back vacantly.

Her taxidermy process having already been completed. It was taking a while for Vincent to finish this for the nine cheerleaders, but he knew in the end it would be worth it. Paige after all was the last one of the squad.

"What did you do to her?", Paige whispered, her voice choked with horror.

"I made her better," Vincent replied, his voice filled with pride. "I preserved her beauty for all time."

Suddenly, it dawned on Paige why her friend wasn't moving. "You... you killed her," Paige spat, her voice laced with disgust.

"No, no I didn't", Vincent paused for a moment, eyeing Maya, "well I guess I did. But it was necessary. It was a sacrifice that had to be made."

"Fuck you," Paige hissed, her eyes flashing in rage.

"Tisk, tisk. Such feisty language, luckily that won't mater for your display. I can make you look far more pleasant and presentable." At this a sadistic smile came upon Vincent's face as he approached his captive.

Paige struggled against her bonds, but they were too strong. There was no escape.

"You're sick," Paige said, her voice filled with anger.

"No, I'm creative," Vincent replied, with amusement. He was now holding a syringe with a green liquid inside, and soon injected it into Paige. She started to feel drowsy, like the world was spinning.

"What did... did you do?", she slurred, her voice weak.

"I just gave you a little something to help with the process," Vincent said with mock concern.

Paige tried to fight it off but was losing badly. She gave it a token effort before collapsing against the table she was strapped to.

"That's it, just relax," Vincent murmured, his voice soothing.

The world around Paige was growing dim, and her thoughts were becoming hazy. She felt as if she were floating on a cloud, and there was nothing to worry about. Slowly she gave into the darkness but swore she could see a single light ahead.

Vincent watched as the Cheer captain expelled her last breath. She was dead and would soon become a permanent fixture. A trophy of his victory. It was time to get to work.

One Week Later

Vincent smiled as he looked at the line up of his nine newest acquisitions. It was nothing personal, they were just beautiful to look at. Despite what some thought, he never used his subjects for more deplorable methods, but rather for pieces of art only.

He looked at Paige O'Hara, the cheer captain's frozen visage forever preserved in a state of defiance, her hair pulled back in a ponytail, and her uniform fitting her snuggly. She was posed with her right hand raised in a fist, her expression fierce.

Maya, the first victim of his newest hunt was positioned next to her captain. Her red hair flowing free, her freckles standing out on her cheeks. She was dressed in her cheer uniform and was bent at the waist, her pompoms in her hands.

The other seven girls were also positioned with their uniforms on, with some in different poses, but were no less impressive. Vincent was quite proud of his work. He had managed to preserve their youth and beauty, and had captured their personalities perfectly, at least in his mind that is.

"What do you think, babe?", he asked, his voice gentle.

"They're perfect," Samantha said, her eyes shining.

"Thank you," Vincent replied, a smile on his

face.

He walked over to his wife and wrapped his arms around her.

"I love you," he whispered, his voice filled with affection.

"I love you, too," Samantha murmured, her voice filled with warmth.

The two kissed, their hearts beating as one. The cheerleaders for their part simply stared forward, not a care in the world. Not that they had the ability to express anything anymore.

CHAPTER 16

Headaches

MAYOR JEFF FREDRICK was having a really bad day, as the so called the pinewood killer appears to have returned. Of course, he denied this to the public, their town was small and couldn't afford to take any hit. It would also certainly ruin plans for his political future if they got wind of what was actually happening. It had been close with that one detective a few years ago that he forced the chief to fire, but still, he seemed to be in the clear, with only conspiracy theories charging him with mismanagement.

For Jeff, this was fine, as few would believe them anyway, and were rather inevitable no mater what he did. If he got this situation under control quietly, he would be president in no time, even it is a bit of an ambitious goal.

"Mr. Mayor, the press is here," said his secretary.

"Shit," the mayor swore, his mood growing worse.

"Mr. Mayor?", his secretary asked, her voice hesitant.

"Tell them I'm busy," Jeff replied, his tone curt.

"But sir," his secretary began.

"I said tell them I'm busy. That's an order," Jeff growled, his eyes flashing with rage.

"Yes, sir", the secretary said before leaving the room.

Jeff was in no condition to talk to the press. He was afraid it might be too late to sweep this all under the rug, this had just been too high profile of an incident. Oh, what was he going to do?

Detective Mark Jameson was pissed. His team had been working nonstop on the case and were making progress. However, the mayor, the fucking mayor, had called the chief, and ordered a complete lockdown of information. He had been a rookie when the last mass disappearances happened in this town, when those Girl Scouts disappeared a few years ago. He remembered one of the detectives at the time drove herself mad due to it and vanished from the face if the earth shortly afterwards. Not that the chief seemed to care, but maybe she was onto something.

It was not the first time this had happened and would not be the last. It was as if the chief was on the mayor's payroll, but the mayor wasn't that dumb, was he? No, the chief was just a coward, and didn't want to piss off the mayor. Jameson couldn't blame him, after all he had the same goal.

He would make the mayor see things his way, and then they would make a real dent in this investigation. Mayor Fredrick had to be rational enough to see that right? He sent a request to the chief earlier this morning asking for federal help in this case, since it was quickly growing out of hand. But to his surprise, he soon got an email denying this request.

"This can't be right," he said, his voice strained.

"What's wrong?", his partner, Detective Amelia Jones asked, her voice concerned.

"I got denied," Jameson said, his voice incredulous.

"What?", Jones exclaimed, her eyes wide.

"Yeah. Apparently, the mayor thinks it's a waste of time and resources," Jameson explained, his voice bitter.

"Are you serious? These are missing

teenagers! What is he thinking?"

"I have no idea. He's either trying to hide something, or is just plain stupid. Either way, we can't let this stand. We need to find these girls, and bring them home," Jameson said, his voice determined.

Detective Jones smiled. "You're starting to sound like detective Collins with those Girl Scouts."

"Who?", Jameson asked, his brow furrowing trying to place the name.

"You know, Sarah Collins. The detective that disappeared a few years ago. Remember, she was the only one willing to dig into this case," Jones said, her voice hesitant. "She got fired due to being too obsessed with it."

"Ahh, right. Yeah, I remember her now. We can't lose sight of our mission. Let's keep going," Jameson replied, his voice firm.

"Right," Jones said, her eyes shining.

With renewed determination, the two detectives got back to work. They would find those girls and would make the mayor regret his decision.

A month later, the girls had not yet been

found. They knew the odds were not likely to find them alive at this point, and the chief was trying to shut down the investigation due to this. It had gotten so bad, that he was threatening to suspend the two detectives if they didn't drop the case.

"This is ridiculous," Jameson seethed, his voice laced with anger.

"I know. The chief has completely lost it," Jones said in sheer disbelief.

"What are we going to do? We can't just let him get away with this," Jameson replied in outrage.

"I don't think there is anything we can do, at least officially", Jones replied.

"Then we do it unofficially", Jameson said with a surge of confidence.

Jones raised an eyebrow. "Careful there, that is the sort of thinking that got Collins fired."

"Yeah, I know. But she was right. Someone needs to put a stop to this," Jameson said, his voice fierce.

"We're not ready for something like that," Jones said, her voice laced with worry.

"Maybe not, but someone has to do something," Jameson replied with a new sense of determination.

"Okay, fine. But we need a plan. We can't just rush in," Jones cautioned.

"I know. I'm open to suggestions," Jameson said,

his tone serious.

The two detectives spent the rest of the day brainstorming, trying to come up with a way to catch the killer, or at least figure out what had happened, even if they couldn't officially do anything about it. Justice would be served, it had to be.

Things were getting ridiculous now. Wherever they went in the search for those girls, they constantly found themselves stonewalled. The chief was insistent there was no case to be found, and forbid any further resources being spent on it. When they tried to blow the whistle and go to the feds, they were rejected, and later found out it had been at the request of the mayor's office. Both Jameson and Jones received a week song suspension as a result of this, which they sure was highly illegal in itself.

They had been back at the precinct for two weeks and had heard nothing. It was as if the case had been completely swept under the rug.

"This is unacceptable," Jones fumed, her voice filled with fury.

"I agree. How could the chief just let this go?", Jameson said, his tone baffled.

"I have no idea. It's like he's under some kind of spell," Jones replied, her voice strained. "Plus, why is the mayor putting up so much resistance for aid?"

Jameson scoffed. "Everyone knows he wants to get out of this town, reach higher office. A serial killer on his watch does not look good on his resume."

Jones nodded. "But the disappearances started under the previous mayor, whose own wife and daughter disappeared."

"Huh, maybe they're not related to this case, and he did it. The guy did resign shortly afterwards, and Mayor Fredrick then came into power as a result."

"Something else to investigate", Jones said coldly.

"We have to find a way to keep the pressure on," Jameson said.

"How? The chief won't listen to us, and the feds are off the table," Jones said, her voice exasperated.

"I guess we're vigilantes then", Jameson shrugged.

"What", Jones exclaimed in surprise, "what do you mean by that?"

"Exactly what I said. We can't sit idly by and let this go," Jameson replied, his eyes burning.

"Are you crazy? We'll get arrested!" Jones said, her eyes wide.

"Not if we do it right," Jameson countered.

"We're not prepared for something like this," Jones said, her voice cautious.

"No, but someone has to do it. It's the right thing, no mater the legality of it." Jameson said this sternly, having already made up his mind.

Jones sighed. "Okay, fine. But we must be careful," she warned.

"Agreed. We can't let anyone know we're involved," Jameson said, his face determined.

"All right. Let's get started," Jones said cautiously.

CHAPTER 17

Shut Down

OF ALL THE THINGS VINCENT Greenwood expected, he did not see the Mayor of Pinehurst physically coming to his taxidermy store in person. Yet here he was, making his way into the shop.

"Well, well, well. What brings the mayor of Pinehurst here, Mr. Fredrick", he said, his tone polite.

"Don't play dumb, Greenwood. I know what you've been up to," the mayor said, his voice stern.

"I'm sorry", Vincent said legitimately confused. "You seem to have had a conversation with yourself that I'm not privy to."

"Cut the crap, Greenwood. You're a dangerous man, and you need to be stopped," the mayor said, his voice laced with authority.

Vincent frowned. "What are you talking

about?"

"Your business, it's full-on disgusting." The mayor then spat on the floor for emphasis.

"Disgusting? I don't understand," Vincent said, his brow furrowing. Mayor Fredrick looked around at the many trophies and displays, his expression one of disdain.

"These things, they're abominations. You can't do this anymore," the mayor said, his voice firm.

Vincent narrowed his eyes. "I'm not going to stop. This is my passion."

"I can't stop you from making them, but I can stop you from selling them. I'm revoking your business license." With that, the mayor slapped a legal looking document on the counter.

Vincent felt a surge of anger and indignation. How dare the mayor try to take his livelihood away?

"You can't do that," Vincent said, his voice laced with venom.

"Yes, I can. And I am in fact doing it. Now, if you don't comply, I'll have no choice but to bring the law down on you," the mayor said, his tone menacing.

Vincent looked like he wanted to strangle the mayor. Instead, he took a deep breath, and composed himself. "Fine. You win," he said, his voice tight.

"Good. I'm glad we could come to an

agreement," the mayor said, a smirk on his face. He then turned on his heel and left the store, accompanied by his bodyguards.

"Why did a mayor of a small-town need bodyguards", Vincent thought to himself as he sadly put up his closed sign. He watched in anger as the mayor's car pulled away. He was going to pay for this.

Susan Fredrick was like any other teenage girl, at least she would be if it weren't for her Dad's job. She was a straight A student, captain of the debate team, and a member of the chess club.

Despite her busy schedule, she somehow always found time to hang out with her friends and enjoy life. She always felt safe, that was her father's goal for Pinehurst after all. The safest, most pleasant town in America. She also knew he had ambitious goals, and wanted to be president one day, and knew that her peace and tranquility would surely come to an end should he accomplish this. Ever since the death of her mother, he seemed to have doubled down on this. She couldn't imagine him leaving her to run for the White House.

She sighed. Her dad was a good man, but

sometimes he could be a bit much. As the daughter of the mayor, she was often dragged into the spotlight, and was expected to behave in a certain manner. She hated it and would sometimes sneak away without telling anyone but her friends, like she was doing now.

She was currently at a pond that only the locals knew about, even though it was public property. She was currently dressed in a red one-piece bathing suit, he long blonde hair in a messy bun. She was with her two best friends, Rachel, and Morgan. They were currently enjoying the summer sun and were overall having a good time.

"This is so relaxing," Rachel sighed, her eyes closed.

"Mmhmm," Morgan agreed, her face serene.

Susan smiled, and laid back on her blanket. The sun was warm, and the breeze was cool. It was the perfect day.

"I love this place. It's so peaceful," Susan said, her voice wistful.

"Yeah, it's the best," Rachel replied, her tone content.

"I could stay here forever," Morgan sighed, her tone dreamy.

"Me, too," Susan said, somewhat sad. All three were going to graduate soon, and then would head off to college, likely different ones at that. This may be one of the last times she sees her best friends.

"I'm going to miss you guys," Rachel said, her voice quiet.

"I'll miss you, too," Morgan said, her voice gentle.

"It's not goodbye yet, we still have time," Susan pointed out.

"I know, but it's still hard," Rachel replied, her voice heavy.

"It's going to be okay," Susan said, her tone reassuring.

"Yeah, we'll still be in touch. This isn't the end," Morgan added, her voice firm.

The girls sat in silence, each lost in their thoughts. They knew that things would change, but they would never let that come between them.

Suddenly a whizzing sound could be heard, followed by a small thunk.

"What was that", Susan asked, not bothering to look up.

"I don't know but—" Another whizzing sound could be heard, followed by another thunk.

Susan sat up, now curious why her friend got cut off. When she took off her sunglasses, she is met by the sight of Rachel and Morgan laying unconscious on the ground.

"What the hell," Susan said, her eyes wide.

Suddenly a third whizzing sound could be heard, along with one more thunk. However, accompanying this was a prick Susan felt in her butt. Suddenly the girl felt sleepy.

"Oh shit," she said, her voice slurred.

She tried to get up, but the drug in her system was too strong. She fell to the ground, her body limp. She was unable to say anything else before the darkness overtook her, and she failed to notice that someone was walking up to her, a hunter of some sort.

Vincent Greenwood whistled a tune as he listened to the radio and pulled into his garage. His hunting trip had been a massive success, and even got some extra game as well.

"Oh, what a day," he murmured, his voice filled with satisfaction.

He stepped out of the van and made his way towards the back. He opened the door and was greeted by the sight of his newest acquisitions, all unconscious, and ready for processing.

"Ahh, there you are," he said, his eyes shining.

He reached into the van and began to load the three girls into a covered cart to bring them into his house without attracting any attention, he wasn't going to risk that. Once done, he carefully pushed the cart through the garage, and into his basement, where his work would begin.

"Oh, yes. I've got big plans for you three," he said, his voice gleeful. He looked at the three girls, his eyes glittering. They were the perfect age and had the ideal bodies. He couldn't wait to start working on them.

"You're going to be beautiful," he whispered, his voice filled with admiration. He leaned down and kissed his primary target, Susan on the forehead. She did not react in the slightest to this.

He removed the three girls from the cart, and began to lay them out on his processing table, where he striped them naked, and started taking measurements. He would poke and prod them, feel them up, all in the name of his art. The girls remained unconscious, unaware of the fate that awaited them. They were in for a long journey, and it was only just beginning.

Vincent admired his three latest masterpieces as he stood in front of them, the three having been lined up to be standing side by side in a line. They were frozen forever in a state of youth and beauty. Susan had been placed in the middle, with Rachel and Morgan to her right and left.

"You're perfect," he murmured, his voice awed.

Vincent stared at their faces, his eyes glimmering. He had captured their personalities perfectly and had given them a new lease on life.

"You'll be safe here. No one will hurt you," he said, his voice gentle. He looked at his collection, his gaze proud. He had created perfection and would protect it with his life. He would never let anything happen to them.

"I promise," he vowed, his voice solemn.

He hoped the mayor learned his lesson, even if he never found out who took his daughter. Had he not done what he did, Vincent would never have hurt Susan, but the mayor would never see it that way.

"I love you," he said, his voice soft. He then kissed Susan's taxidermied form on her cold still lips, causing the poor girl to wobble in place. With one final look, he walked away, his heart filled with pride. His collection was growing, and he couldn't be happier. He had taken the mayor's daughter, and nothing could bring him down.

CHAPTER 18

Corruption

MAYOR FREDRICK WAS at the end of his rope. It had been three months since his daughter had gone missing, and there was still no trace of her. Was this retribution for what he had down about those other cases? No, it couldn't be, he didn't believe in that sort of thing. He only believes in power and those who have it, and he had it. There had to be some other reason.

He was sitting at his desk in his office, a stack of paperwork in front of him. He had a mountain of the stuff to deal with but just couldn't concentrate.

"Fuck it," he muttered, "I'll call the fucking feds."

He reached for the phone, his hand trembling. He needed help, and the FBI were the only ones he could trust.

He dialed the number and waited. The phone

rang twice before someone picked up.

"Hello?", a man's voice answered.

"Hello, I need your help," the mayor said, his voice strained.

"Sorry sir, you have the wrong number," the man replied, his voice apologetic.

"I'm sorry, do you know who this is?" The phone line clicked as the other person hung up.

Mayor Fredrick sat there for a moment, stunned. Did the FBI just hang up on him?

"What the fuck," he muttered, his eyes wide. He was about to dial again when his intercom buzzed.

"Mayor Fredrick, there's a detective Jameson and Detective Jones here to see you," his secretary said.

"Send them in," the mayor replied, his voice weary. A few moments later, the two detectives came in, their expressions grim.

"Welcome, welcome," the mayor said, putting on a false smile. "I take it you have news about Susan?"

"Err......... no, not exactly", Detective Jones said tersely.

The mayor raised an eyebrow. "Then why are you here?"

"We need to ask you some questions," Jameson replied, his tone serious.

"About what?", the mayor asked, his voice wary.

"About the missing person cases", detective Jameson said. "All of the missing person cases."

"Now those aren't important, what is important is Susan", Mayor Fredrick said exasperated.

"They're related," Jones said, her voice confident.

"What? How?", the mayor asked, his tone incredulous.

"We have reason to believe the Pinehurst killer is back," Jameson replied, his voice grave.

The mayor stared at the two deceives for a moment before uttering the words, "get out."

"Excuse me?", Jones asked, her voice laced with indignation.

"I said get out. You're wasting my time," the mayor said, his tone angry.

"Sir, we have reason to believe that this killer may be involved. Everything seems to point to them taking Susan on purpose to get back at you."

"Bullshit," the mayor spat, his eyes flashing.

"It's the truth to the best of our knowledge, sir," Jameson said, his voice earnest.

The mayor narrowed his eyes. "Read. My. Lips. There is no serial killer in this town. Pinehurst is a nice community."

Jones and Jameson exchanged a glance, unsure what to do. They hadn't expected this reaction from the mayor, especially when it concerned his own daughter.

"Sir, with all due respect, we have a job to do. We need to investigate the possibility," Jameson said, his voice respectful.

"Perhaps even call the feds in."

The mayor scoffed, "they hung up on me."

"What? Why would they do that?", Jones asked, her tone bewildered.

"Are you sure you called the right number?"

"Yes, I am sure, and I don't know. They've been giving me the run around lately," the mayor said, his voice strained. Granted he had only tried once to call them, and never actually confirmed it was the right number, but they didn't need to know that.

"Maybe it's time to accept the truth. There's a killer in Pinehurst, and it's time we face that reality," Jameson said, his tone somber.

"Didn't I tell you to get out? You can bet the chief is going to hear about this."

"Sir, we're just trying to do our jobs," Jones said, her voice defensive.

"And I'm trying to do mine. Now leave," the mayor ordered.

"Yes, sir," Jameson said, his voice stiff.

"Of course, sir", Jones said, turning to leave herself.

Once the two detectives left, Mayor Fredrick walked to his liquor cabinet and poured himself a drink.

"There is no killer in Pinehurst. There couldn't be, otherwise all his plans will be ruined. He couldn't have a killer on his hands. He couldn't."

The next day, the two detectives were summoned to the chief's office. They knew that the mayor must have complained and were prepared for the worst.

"Ah, Detectives Jameson and Jones. I wish this meeting was under better circumstances."

"Sir?" both detectives asked at the same time.

"I had an interesting call from the mayor last night. The man was drunk as a skunk, but it was interesting none the less", the chief said, a hint of annoyance in his voice.

"What... did he say?", Jameson asked, his voice cautious.

"He said that the two of you are a threat to the safety of the town. That you are obsessed with the so called 'pinewood killer', and are ignoring the case of his missing daughter," the chief replied, his tone exasperated.

Jones rolled her eyes. "That's not true, sir."

"Is that so? Because from where I'm standing, you have ignored the mayor's request to close the other investigations and haven't given priority to that of his daughters."

"We're just trying to get to the bottom of the matter, sir," Jameson said, his tone defensive.

The chief sighed. "I'm sorry, but I'm going to have to put you two on administrative leave."

"Sir", Jones exclaimed, her eyes bulging.

"Don't give me that, Amelia. I know you think I'm being unreasonable, but the mayor has made his position clear. He wants you two off the case."

"What about Susan?", Jameson asked, his voice heated.

"I will make finding her my top priority. You can trust me on that," the Chief said. Neither of them truly believed this.

Jones looked at her partner, her expression grim. "And if we continue those other cases on our own dime?" He asked the chief.

The chief gave the two detectives a stern look. "Amelia, Mark. You can't interfere in this case... or any of them. The mayor made that clear, and he has the full backing of the city council. You will be fired if you try."

"Very well." Jameson said coldly. This was the only thing he could say.

"Thank you for understanding. I'm sorry it had to come to this," the chief said, his tone sickly sweet as if talking down to a child.

"I am too," Jameson replied, his voice grim.

The two then left the office together in order to gather their things.

"So now what?" Jones asked her partner.

Jameson shook his head. "I don't know. This is insane. The mayor is trying to cover up a serial killer."

Jones looked at Jameson, her expression pensive. "What if we're wrong?

Jameson scoffed. "I doubt it at this point. Though we'll probably get formally fired anyway."

Jones sighed. "Yeah, you're right. What do we do now?"

Jameson shook his head. "I don't know. Maybe the national media, take the mayor and chief down with us?"

"Maybe, but I doubt it would go well," Jones said, her tone filled with worry.

"I know, but what other choice do we have?", Jameson asked.

"I don't know, but we need to figure it out," Jones said, her tone urgent.

"Yeah, let's go get some coffee. We can talk more then," Jameson said, his voice tired. The two then left the station for what they felt would be the last time.

The media reaction to the case certainly turned heads and did in fact get the two detectives fired from their jobs. The mayor though, somehow, he slipped through everything, and put the blame on the two now former detectives. Eventually people got bored of the story and moved on to other greater things in the moment. But for the two detectives, this was all they were left with. Now they were both jobless, facing eviction, and filled with anger.

"This isn't over," Jameson seethed. The two were currently at his apartment, trying to come up with a plan.

"I know, but what can we do? We're powerless," Jones said, her voice frustrated.

"At this point, I don't care", Jameson said. "I'm leaving this town and heading to New York to start over."

"New York, huh?", Jones said, her tone thoughtful.

"Yeah. I've always wanted to go there," Jameson said, his expression wistful.

"It sounds good. Can I come with you? Also, what about the killer?"

"Yes, you can, and If we find him and he promises to make the mayor and chiefs life hell, I'm tempted to let him be." Jameson did not hide his anger and contempt for the two men.

"Seriously, you would make that deal with a

serial killer?"

"Yes, I would. I hate those two scumbags that much. Also, I would make them promise not to kill anymore."

"Sounds a bit flimsy, but yeah, I guess you're right," Jones said, her tone defeated.

"We'll find him," Jameson said with a renewed confidence.

"Yeah, but how? He's covered his tracks too well," Jones said, her voice bitter.

"I have one more lead to visit. I went through Collins notes before we got kicked out of the station and found that she was obsessed with this taxidermy shop."

Jones raised an eyebrow. "The one that closed down?"

"Yeah, the one shut down personally by our illustrious mayor," Jameson said, his voice grim.

"That can't be a coincidence, right?" Jones asked, raising an eyebrow.

"No, it can't be," Jameson replied, his face set in a frown. "It's just not enough to do an actual investigation on."

"But it's a start," Jones said, her eyes gleaming.

"Yeah, let's do it," Jameson said.

The two then left Jameson's apartment, their mission clear. It was time to confront the Pinehurst killer.

CHAPTER 19

Frame Up

VINCENT GREENWOOD WAS having a bad day. The media descending upon Pinehurst in search of a killer proved to be both a blessing and a curse. On the one hand, it meant that the mayor was desperate, which would likely result in his demise. On the other hand, it brought a lot of unwanted attention to his home, and that could spell disaster.

However, he was surprised at how long it had lasted, not very. The media had found something else to obsess about, and the mayor had gotten away with his coverup. His reputation was ruined, but he still held all the power. It was infuriating, and Vincent wanted nothing more than to expose the mayor and ruin him. He was just not sure how to go about it.

He was currently sitting at his kitchen table,

a cup of coffee in his hand. His wife Samantha was currently doing the dishes. They had burgers made up of Susan Fredrick's remaining flesh, she had been delicious.

"Damn, I was hoping the media would have gotten wind of what happened," Vincent muttered.

"Me, too. I can't believe the mayor got away with it," Samantha said, her voice angry. "What do you think about moving elsewhere."

"I don't know. It might be worth considering," Vincent replied, his tone thoughtful.

"Maybe California. It's far enough away from the east coast, but still a popular destination" Samantha suggested. "Plus lots of people are leaving because of the 'killer' on the loose. In a year, this place will be a ghost town."

"It's getting our trophies there that's the problem. Also, I don't want the mayor to win."

Samantha smiled. "So, one last hurrah so to speak before leaving?"

"Yeah, let's do it. Fuck the mayor," Vincent said, his voice filled with conviction.

Samantha's smile grew wider. "I like the sound of that." Suddenly, the doorbell rang.

Vincent raised an eyebrow. "Were you expecting anyone?" "No, you?", Samantha asked.

"Nope," Vincent replied. He stood up and

went to answer the door. He opened it and found himself face to face with two rather disheveled people, a man and a woman.

"Hello," Vincent asked his tone wary.

"Hello, Mr. Greenwood. My name is Amelia Jones, and this is Mark Jameson. We're looking for the Pinehurst killer," the woman, Amelia said, her tone businesslike. "And we know it's you."

Vincent was shocked and took a moment to collect his thoughts. "I'm sorry, what?"

"You're the one behind the killings. We have proof," Amelia replied, her voice calm.

"And if I was the killer, why wouldn't I just kill you then," Vincent asked, wondering what their endgame was.

"Because we're not officers of the law anymore, and rather hate the chief and mayor", Jameson said, his voice obviously bitter. "And I suspect you do as well... at least the mayor anyway."

This surprised Vincent, and was suddenly interested in what they wanted to say. "Why don't you come in", he said, stepping to the side. The two former detectives then entered the home, the door closing behind them.

It was late afternoon, and the sun was setting. Mark and Amelia were seated on a couch in the Greenwoods living room, their expressions grim.

"So, you two have proof, huh?", Vincent said, his tone curious.

"Well, it is rather obvious if any one actually bothered to look via process of elimination", Jones explained.

Vincent looked taken back by this. Was he really that obvious? "And how do I know this is not a sting operation and that you are not wearing a wire?"

"You want us to strip naked?" Jameson asked.

"Um, no. I think we can skip that," Vincent said, though his expression was amused.

"I thought so," Amelia said, her voice wry.

"So, what exactly do you have against the mayor and chief of Police?", Vincent asked, his tone cautious.

"They're a pair of corrupt bastards. The mayor has been covering up murders, your murders, and the chief has been covering for him," Amelia said, her tone filled with disdain.

"Really? That's interesting," Vincent said, his voice neutral.

"It is, isn't it?", Jones said, her expression pensive.

"So, what do you want from me? You know,

assuming I actually am the killer."

"We want to frame the chief and the Mayor. You see the writing on the wall on what's happening to this town right?" Jones said, admonished.

"Yes, I do," Vincent replied, his voice somber.

"If we work together, we can take them down," Amelia said, her tone hopeful. "You can 'retire' from your activities in peace, no one the wiser. Unless of course... you have no plans on stopping.

Vincent was silent for a moment as he contemplated her offer. He did consider retiring from his hunting, especially after the loss of his business. He doubted he could continue his work in California without attracting attention to himself.

"All right, I'm in. What do you have in mind?", Vincent asked, his voice curious.

Amelia smiled knowingly. "So, you are the killer then?"

"Oh fuck," Vincent said as he realized his mistake.

"Relax, we're not here to arrest you. We're on your side," Amelia said, her voice soothing.

Vincent let out a breath he didn't know he was holding. "Sorry, I'm a bit paranoid."

"Don't worry, we understand," Jameson said, his tone reassuring.

"So, what's the plan?", Vincent asked, his

expression eager to take down the mayor.

"We have a few ideas", Jones said smiling devilishly. "Well probably go to hell for it, but it should work."

"What kind of ideas?", Vincent asked, his voice cautious.

"We were thinking of framing the mayor and the chief by setting them up to take the fall for the killings," Jameson said, his tone matter- of-factly.

"I'm listening", Vincent said, now smiling himself.

"Now, no one else can know what you are about to see", Vincent said as he led the two former detectives down a secret passageway. Against his better judgement, as well as Samantha's, Vincent had decided to trust Jones and Jameson. He didn't know why, but he had a gut feeling they were telling the truth. When they asked what happened to his prey, he felt an urge to show them off, something he had only ever done with Samantha.

"Where are you taking us?", Amelia asked, her voice filled with anticipation.

"You'll see," Vincent replied, his tone cryptic.

"I hope you're not planning on killing us," Jameson joked, his voice nervous.

"Of course not. If I wanted to kill you, I would have done it by now," Vincent said, his voice dry.

"Good to know," Jones muttered.

After a few minutes of walking, the group arrived at a hidden room. Vincent then turned on he lights, illuminated dozens of figures on display throughout it.

"Holy shit," Jameson breathed.

"Impressive, isn't it?", Vincent said, his voice smug.

"You could say that" Jones murmured, her eyes wide as she looked at a Girl Scout forever selling cookies.

"How long have you been doing this?" Jameson asked as he looked down a cheerleader who forever was doing a scale pose.

"I was in an accident a few years ago, a girl got killed, and I didn't want to go to jail. So, I covered it up, brought her body home, and turned her into a trophy." As Vincent said this, he longingly looked at the frozen form of Emily Lyon, who was still jogging after all of these years. "It just kind of went out of control after that."

Jones and Jameson were both stunned into silence. They couldn't believe their eyes. It was like they had stepped into a morbid art museum.

"Well, this is quite a collection," Jameson said, his voice shaky.

"It's my life's work," Vincent said, his voice wistful.

I can see that," Amelia said, her voice awed.

"I hope you're not planning on adding us to it," Jameson said, his voice uneasy.

Vincent smiled. "Well, if this plan of ours works, you can consider me retired. I have a family now to take care of, and don't have much time for this. That, and I'm just getting older." Vincent said this last part sadly.

"That's good to hear," Jones said, her voice relieved.

"Yeah, it's nice to meet a serial killer with a heart," Jameson said, his tone amused.

"I'm not a serial killer. I'm a hunter."

"Potato, potatoe", Jones said indifferent to the distinction.

"They feel awfully light", Jameson asked as he picked up a sitting Girl Scout who had been known as Emily in her former life.

"That's because I removed their internals. It makes them lighter and easier to transport," Vincent explained, his tone casual.

"Clever," Jameson murmured, his expression pensive.

"Thank you," Vincent replied, his voice filled with Pride.

"What did you do with the internal organs?", Jones asked, her tone curious.

"I ate them," Vincent said, his tone not missing a beat.

"You did?", Jones said, her eyes widening.

"Yup. They were delicious," Vincent replied, his voice not showing regret.

Jameson looked at him, his expression horrified. This bothered him much more than the killing and stuffing on his victims, but a thought suddenly came to him. "We could use that. Well not the eating part."

"What are you talking about?", Vincent asked, his voice confused.

"What if we plant some of the remains you don't use in the mayor's and chief's houses", Jameson asked, his expression devious. "Then submit an anonymous tip to the FBI."

Vincent thought about this for a moment before nodding his head. "That could work. Though I am fresh out of remains at the moment."

"Shit, we're definitely going to hell", Jones said as she realized the implications of this. She would never admit to this later, but the prospect of framing the chief and the mayor for murder did bring her a dark sense of pleasure.

"Oh, well," Vincent said, his voice amused. "I'll try to find someone who 'deserved it' so to speak."

Jones and Jameson looked at each other nervous. What did they exactly get themselves into?

CHAPTER 20

Execution

MAYOR FREDRICK HAD all but given up hope that Susan would ever be found alive. There was no trace of her, and the media circus was finally leaving. All he could do was wait, and hope for the best.

He was currently in his office, working on his campaign for congress. Despite the bad press, in his mind, all news was good news. He could use Susan's disappearance after all to gain sympathy from the voters.

His intercom buzzed, causing him to look up from his campaign materials "Mayor Fredrick, you have a visitor," his secretary said, her voice strained.

"Who is it?"

Before he could get an answer, the mayor's door suddenly was kicked down, with an FBI response team suddenly pouring into the room.

A black FBI agent suddenly sauntered in, and was rather calm.

"Jefferson Fredrick, you're under arrest for conspiracy, and being an accessory to murder. You have the right to remain silent. Anything you say can and will be used against you in a court of law. You have the right to an attorney. If you cannot afford an attorney, one will be appointed for you," the agent said, his voice flat.

The mayor could only stare, his eyes wide and mouth agape. "What... what are you talking about", he asked as he was being handcuffed.

"You've been implicated in the serial killings that have been happening in Pinehurst," the agent replied, his voice cold. "We found human remains in your home."

"Why were you in my home."

"We got a rather interesting tip to take a look for evidence of a killer there."

"But that's ridiculous! There's no killer! I've done nothing wrong!"

"Seriously, have you been living under a rock? Take him away", the agent said.

"But I have a campaign to run!"

"Not anymore," the agent replied, his voice smug.

The mayor could only watch in stunned silence as he was escorted out of his office, his political career in ruins. Meanwhile across town at the police station, the chief of police was barricaded in his office. He was sweating bullets as the FBI tried to coax him out of there.

"Chief, please come out. We just want to talk," an agent called out, his voice soothing.

"Fuck you!" the chief shouted, his voice hysterical.

"Look, if you come out, we can talk this out. You'll get a fair trial, and everything will be fine," the agent promised.

The chief didn't know why they were here to arrest him, but he suspected it had to do with certain odd finances or photos on his computer. How could he have messed that up. He looked at his gun on his belt. It was fully loaded. Did he dare? His life was over either way, and he would never survive in prison.

"Come on, you're only making this harder on yourself," the agent said, his tone patient.

The chief sighed, his shoulders slumping. He had no choice. "All right, I'm coming out," he said, his voice resigned.

As the chief walked out of the office, he stopped in the doorway and pulled out his pistol. Before anyone could react, he raised the gun to his head and pulled the trigger.

The shot was deafening, and everyone stood in stunned silence as the chief fell to the floor, a bullet hole in his forehead.

"Shit, what the fuck just happened?", an agent said, his eyes wide.

"I don't know, but we're going to need a cleaning crew," the lead agent replied, his voice weary.

"Jesus Christ. What a clusterfuck," another agent muttered, shaking his head.

"You can say that again," the lead agent said grimly.

Across town, Vincent Greenwood was keeping himself busy. This would be his final trophy, his magnum opus. The mayor and the chief were both set to be gone, and Pinehurst would soon be abandoned. It was time for him to retire and focus on his family.

Vincent was currently in his workshop, building the frame for his next masterpiece. She had been an actress named Mila Black, a pretty brunette and former child actress. He and his coconspirators had taken her a week ago and planted some of her flesh in the mayor's and chiefs' fridges that morning, along with some of her clothes. One anonymous tip to the FBI, and the rest was history.

As Vincent worked, he couldn't help but smile. All he had to do was finish the frame, and his masterpiece would be complete.

Carefully, he placed the actresses face onto the head of the frame, the brown glass eyes staring back at him. Even with just her face, she looked very realistic already.

Vincent stepped back and admired his work, his smile growing wider. She was perfect and would be the centerpiece of his collection.

With a satisfied nod, he went to work on the body, the actress's voice forever lost to time. Several hours later, his masterpiece was completed. She was perfect, a frozen beauty for him to admire forever.

Vincent then carried the actress into the dining room, her glass eyes staring into space.

"There, that's better," he said, his voice satisfied.

"She's beautiful," Samantha said, her voice awed.

"Thanks, love," Vincent replied, his voice filled with pride. He thought for a few moments before kissing Samantha. It was the best kiss they had shared outside of their wedding.

"This is a new beginning," Samantha said, her voice hopeful.

"Yeah, I can't believe we actually pulled it off," Vincent said, his voice filled with disbelief.

Samantha laughed. "Yeah, it's surreal."

Vincent sighed. "We should get out of here soon. Once people start leaving, the feds will likely come snooping around."

"Yeah, that's true. Do you have everything packed?", Samantha asked, her tone concerned.

"I think so," Vincent replied, his voice thoughtful. "Just the trophies are left."

Samantha smiled. "Well, let's get to it. I can't wait to start our new lives in California."

Vincent nodded. "Yeah, me too."

The two then began the long task of packing up their trophies and preparing for their move.

As the couple worked, they couldn't help but feel a sense of accomplishment. Not only had they escaped justice, but they had also gotten revenge on the mayor and the chief. It was a bittersweet feeling, but one that was worth it.

A white sedan that did not appear out of the ordinary was making its way out of town, destination, New York City. Their plan had worked perfectly, the bastard chief and mayor were taken down, and they solved the mystery of the Pinehurst killer, not that anyone knew that part. They were headed to the big apple for a new life.

"I still can't believe it worked," Amelia Jones said, her tone amazed.

"I know, it's crazy. But it's also kind of sad," Mark Jameson said, his voice wistful.

"Yeah, I guess so," Amelia replied, her tone somber. "But hey, we made the world a safer place. That's got to count for something," Mark said, his voice optimistic.

They had convinced the Pinehurst killer to retire from his activities at the cost of only one more life. That had to be worth something in karma, right?

Amelia smiled. "Yeah, you're right. We did good."

"Yeah, we did," Mark replied, his voice filled with conviction.

The couple continued to drive in silence, their thoughts filled with their actions and what they had done.

They knew they would have to live with their decisions, what they knew, and the consequences of their actions, but they were okay with that. After all, they had made the world a better place, and that was what really mattered.

"We did the right thing, right", Jameson asked aloud.

Jones thought for a moment. "Yeah, we did. There was no other way."

The two sat in silence for the rest of their trip to New York.

In New York City, Amelia Jones and Mark Jameson were also settling into their new home. It was a modest apartment in the city, and it was a far cry from the one they left behind. The two former partners decided to room together until they could get back on their feet and start their new lives.

"This place is great," Amelia said, her voice filled with awe. "But small though."

"Well, it's New York City, what did you expect?" Mark asked sarcastically.

"I don't know. I'm just so excited," Amelia replied, her voice giddy.

"Me, too. This is the start of a new chapter in our lives," Mark said, his voice determined.

"Do you feel bad that we let a killer get away, like it goes against everything we ever stood for", Amelia asked.

"Nah, I'm fine with it. He's retired, and we took down the corrupt bastards. I'd say that's a win," Mark replied, his voice matter-of-fact. "Besides, you read what else they found at the chiefs house. What we did was a necessary evil."

"You're right," Amelia said, her tone resigned.

Mark nodded. "Now, let's get unpacked. I can't wait to explore the city."

"Yeah, me, too," Amelia replied, her voice excited.

With that, the two set to work unpacking their belongings, their hearts full of hope for the future.

Former Mayor Jefferson Fredrick found himself charged with the murder of actress Mila Black, and despite a lack of physical evidence, also found guilty for several of the 'Pinehurst killer' murders, or at least held in contempt of them. He was sentenced to life in prison without the possibility of parole.

The chief was posthumously convicted in the court of public opinion, and was buried next to his wife, a woman who had committed suicide herself several years earlier. The media circus around the case had died down, and the town was slowly but surely emptying.

In a few years, the once thriving town would be all but abandoned. With the death of the chief and arrest of the mayor, no more killing's happened, which convinced people they were the true killers. They had not only wrongfully lost in the court of law, but in the court of public opinion as well.

Amelia and Mark both kept in touch with Vincent and Samantha, the four having become friends over the course of their ordeal. They never spoke about what happened, but there was an unspoken understanding between them. They would keep each other's secrets, and they would live out their lives in peace. It was a strange situation, but one that seemed to work for them. No one would know their secrets. A great reset had happened, and they would live in peace from then on.

EPILOGUE

THE DOOR TO THE MOVING truck opened for the first time in several days after a cross country journey. Inside were all the worldly possessions of the Greenwood family; furniture, cribs, kitchen appliances, and carefully wrapped in plastic taxidermied human trophies.

It had been a harrowing journey, but they were finally in their new home.

"Oh, my God, it's perfect," Samantha gushed, her voice filled with excitement.

"Yeah, I love it," Vincent agreed, his voice awed.

The home was colonial revival style and was located in Napa Valley. The two planned to leave their taxidermied days behind them and go into wine making. Obviously they would keep their current trophies, at least in a hidden room in the basement.

"I can't believe we're actually here,"

Samantha said, her voice disbelieving.

"Me, too," Vincent replied, his voice filled with wonder. The two then got to work unpacking their belongings, their future bright.

They had no idea what lay ahead, but they were excited for the new life they were going to start. And with their newfound freedom, they were ready for anything.

Vincent would keep to his word and was officially retired from human hunting and trophy making. The last few weeks had been a whirlwind, but he felt content. He would be starting over and was happy for it.

ABOUT THE AUTHOR

Joey Dolton

Joey Dolton is a captivating wordsmith with a penchant for exploring the uncharted realms of emotions and fear, and is a versatile author who seamlessly weaves the threads of romance, science fiction, and horror into a tapestry of gripping narratives. Born with a vivid imagination and an insatiable curiosity, Joey's literary journey has been marked by a fearless exploration of the human experience within the extraordinary

BOOKS BY THIS AUTHOR

Time Freeze

Eighteen year-old Mark Donovan is about to discover the extraordinary power within himself. Unbeknownst to Mark, his life is about to take a thrilling turn as he uncovers a mysterious ability to freeze time—unraveling the fabric of reality in the most enchanting way.

"Time Freeze" follows Mark as he navigates the delicate balance between the ordinary and the extraordinary. Mark's journey begins when he accidentally freezes time during a seemingly routine day, revealing a hidden realm where seconds stretch into eternity and the world becomes his canvas. As Mark learns to wield this newfound power, he discovers the limitless possibilities that come with manipulating time.

Printed in Great Britain
by Amazon